The Last Time

I Smelled

Lavender Tea

For Deedad

Prologue

Mid July, 1987

The clouds formed a dark, grey blanket over the Massachusetts sky which made the afternoon appear like night. Thunder and lightning soon clashed together above the empty, rain-soaked highway that meandered along a steep mountain. It remained empty until a silver Plymouth Voyager minivan appeared travelling down it. The vehicle passed by a sign that said the next exit was Parkfield.

Inside the minivan was the Sinclair family, a dad, a mom and their daughter. They watched the menacing storm, each of them anticipating the next sudden bolt of lightning as the rain came down in sheets. The dad sat up in his seat and drove with total concentration. His wife, who sat next to him, played with the radio trying to find a station that did not involve static. Their daughter, a thirteen-year-old girl named Ava, sat in the back seat moving her finger along with the raindrops that ran across her window as if she were controlling their movements.

"Will we see the moon tonight, Dad?" Ava asked.

"No, I'm afraid not through these clouds. It's too bad because it's a blood moon. They only happen every few years."

Thunder boomed seemingly right over the minivan.

"William, we need to pull over. The storm doesn't look like it's going to clear up any time soon," Ava's mother said as she grabbed her hot tea from one of the cupholders and took a sip.

"We are almost there, honey. The next exit is Parkfield," he shot back, tensely focused on the road.

"Could I have some, Mom?" Ava requested.

"Lavender tea? I don't think you'll like it, but okay. You may take to it when you get older and go off to college. You know, like Harvard!" she turned in her seat to hand her daughter the tea.

"Belle, don't pressure her. She can go to college wherever she wants."

"I know, but I think she's smart enough to get into Harvard," Belle said as she watched Ava taste the slightly minty, sweet liquid.

"So? What do you think?" her mother asked.

"It's very good," Ava said as she handed the cup back to her mother.

They approached the Parkfield exit and began travelling down a winding, two-lane road. It wasn't long before they saw a bright green sign that read *Welcome to Parkfield.*

"Parkfield!" Ava said enthusiastically.

"Why are we going here again?" Belle asked William.

"As I told you, I have ancestors that lived here and I thought we could learn more about them if we visited. Besides the hotel has a pool and free HBO!"

"Oh, alright," the mother took another sip of her tea and watched the dark sky. Thunder boomed again.

"Ava, are you still wearing the necklace I gave you?" her father inquired.

"Yes, Dad." Ava looked at the necklace around her neck that was given to her on her thirteenth birthday The oddly shaped purple stone on it seemed to glow a little; it was a pretty and comforting sight.

"Make sure to take care of that and don't lose it. It's a family heirloom, you know."

"I know, I'll keep it safe."

The downpour made the road difficult to see, and William found himself swerving on the slippery road.

"Watch out!" Belle hollered.

"I got it," William said as he slowed down and drove steadier.

"You almost ran off the road!"

"But I didn't, Belle, we're okay. Right, Ava?"

Ava was distracted as she looked behind her seat. Two bright headlights grew bigger and bigger as they rapidly approached their minivan.

"There's a car coming," Ava stated.

"What?" Belle asked.

"A car," Ava continued to gaze behind her, "It's getting really close to us!"

The mother turned around in her seat and suddenly saw the glare of headlights flood through the rear window.

"William, look out!" Belle screamed.

It was too late. A sudden jolt to the back of the minivan resulted in it spinning out of control. It tumbled off the road, down a steep cliff and into a ditch. Rain plummeted and thunder crashed once more as the minivan sat motionless. Ava looked around startled. The smell of lavender tea was strong as it had spilled all over.

"Mom? Dad?" Ava said as she tapped on their shoulders. They didn't move.

"Wake up, please!"

Her parents were slumped over in their seats motionless. Ava leaned back in her seat feeling increasingly weak. Somehow, the radio was now on a station that came in clearly.

"And that was Whitney Houston's newest song: 'I Wanna Dance with Somebody'. Just a reminder we are still under a severe thunderstorm warning, so to all those who are on the roadways, please drive cautiously..."

"Mom...Dad...." Ava said again in a weakened whisper. Then she started hearing voices outside of the wrecked vehicle.

Within seconds, multiple tall figures appeared outside the van's windows. They wore what looked like black, hooded robes.

She clutched the stone that was attached to her necklace and cried for she knew that this might be the end.

The strange men crept to the front of the van where her parents sat and were about to break in when Ava suddenly felt dizzy and began blacking out.

Death was a concept so frightening that she couldn't imagine bearing it. Peace and death were two words she believed were complete opposites, which was why the idea of dying was a horrifying one. She didn't want to die, nor did she want to leave this world and its many gifts. But she knew that the end was inevitable, so she closed her eyes and let the moment take her.

Chapter One

"An eighty percent chance of rain is expected until six here in the city. No accidents have been reported yet but drive with caution as the rain is likely to get heavier. Next up is the classic Whitney Houston song 'I Wanna Dance with Somebody' here on WCMA."

Besides the Whitney Houston song in the background, Ava drove in silence. Drops of rain soon began to hit her windshield and she quickly turned on her wipers. The day was light-grey and boring, but it was the beginning of summer, so she was headed to her uncle's apartment after her first year at Harvard.

It was six years after the car crash, which made her nineteen years old. Her parents died on that day. She tried to not think about it, but every raindrop reminded her of right before the incident, and every clap of thunder reminded her of the crash itself.

Ava turned off the radio and drove in complete silence. Her first year at Harvard was a crazy blur and she was longing for a break back home with Uncle Matthew, her father's brother and her legal guardian.

She loved being raised by her uncle, from playing cards all day to going to the police station to see what types of cases he had solved during his career as a detective. Spending time with her uncle is one of the few things she looks forward to in life—besides becoming a world-renowned author.

Becoming an author was something Ava promised her parents, and she has worked to live up to that promise by trying to write every day.

Within minutes, she arrived at her uncle's apartment complex which was right off of the highway exit. Cars passed by with their bright headlights as Ava pulled into the almost empty parking lot. The rain fell heavier, she wanted to get inside quickly. She opened the trunk and retrieved her suitcase before scampering inside the lobby area the off-white painted building.

The place was dry and quiet. Gentle music played from a radio somewhere. An old lady Ava had never seen before sat behind the lobby desk reading a magazine. Her hair was frizzy and gray, she wore a flowered vest and white reading glasses that slipped down her nose every few seconds before she pushed them back up again with her finger.

The walls were a light orange, like the color of one of those push-up popsicles. There was a painting of a fat cat that hung on the wall behind the desk, leering over the room as if it owned the place. The elevator was located at the very back of the room, so Ava picked up her suitcase and began heading that way. It wasn't until she was about to walk past the desk when the woman spoke.

"Where do you think you're going young lady?" she asked in an uptight tone.

"Matthew Sinclair's apartment. Matthew's my uncle, I used to live here with him," Ava said.

"How old are you?" the lady set down her magazine and folded her arms.

"Nineteen…" Ava glanced around, hoping someone would walk in or come out of the elevator.

"You don't look old enough to be nineteen," the old lady scoffed.

"Oh, okay," Ava said.

"What's your name?" the old lady demanded.

"Ava…"

Ava started toward the elevator again, but the old lady got up and stepped in her path.

"Hold up! Don't try to get by me! Listen here, Eva, I don't appreciate your attitude, and if you continue to harass me like this, I'll call the police."

"Harass you? I didn't do anything! I just want to visit my uncle!" Ava stammered, "Besides, my uncle is with the po—"

As if on cue, the elevator doors opened and out walked Uncle Matthew. He wore a buttoned up Hawaiian shirt and khaki shorts. He saw Ava and beamed.

"Ava!" he said running over to hug her.

"You know this girl?" the old woman snarked, pushing her glasses up to the top of her nose again.

"Why, yes, Debra, this is my niece. She lives here with me when she's not at school."

"Hmph," Debra said as she rolled her eyes and returned to her desk.

"I'm so glad you're here, come on!" Uncle Matthew smiled and grabbed her suitcase. As Ava followed, she took one more glance at the woman behind the desk, who glared at Ava from her magazine.

Ava entered the elevator alongside her uncle as he pressed the button for the fifth floor. The elevator shook a little before slowly rising to their destination.

"She's new," Ava noted, "is she always like that?"

"Debra? Always," Uncle Matthew said.

"And you haven't asked her out yet?" Ava joked.

"Yeah, right."

Ava chuckled as the elevator dinged and the doors slowly opened to reveal a long, stark white hallway filled with beige doors. Numbers were nailed onto each door, 108, 109, and so on. They passed each one until they reached 115 at the end of the hall.

"Here we are, home sweet home," Uncle Matthew said as he unlocked and pushed open the door.

Maybe there was a new plant on his coffee table, or a new picture in his display of picture frames on the wall, but other than that, nothing had really changed since Ava moved in with him after her parents passed away. The apartment was small but cozy, with soft white walls and hardwood floors. There were two bedrooms, a bathroom, a kitchen and living room. It was humble, but Matthew did his best to keep the place tidy and make it feel like a home.

Ava walked inside and looked at the portraits that hung on the wall next to the kitchen. Some were pictures of her and her uncle, while others showed images of Uncle Matthew standing in front of different police stations, usually giving a thumbs up and a lighthearted smile. And, of course, there were family pictures of her father and mother with Matthew as well. Ava lightly touched the different frames, smiling at each image as she walked past the collection of pictures.

She walked into the living room and approached one of the windows. Outside, she looked at the highway with cars that zoomed by and rain that pattered upon every object. The sky continued to grow darker until streetlights suddenly turned on in the parking lot. Under one streetlight, a solitary man stood. The sight of the man took Ava back for a moment. She tried to find a face, but he was cloaked in a dark hood. Ava watched the man from the window for several minutes waiting for him to make some kind of move, but he just stood there motionless in the rain. The idea of a man watching her uncle's apartment building from outside freaked her out a little. She couldn't look away until finally Uncle Matthew spoke.

"So, put your stuff in your bedroom, and I'm gonna fix dinner," Uncle Matthew said from the kitchen. "I have mac n' cheese and cereal. What'll it be?"

"Um, cereal," Ava replied, looking away from the window.

"Rice Krispies?" Uncle Matthew asked as he retrieved two bowls from one of the cabinets.

"Mhm," Ava replied and quickly focused her eyes back to the man under the streetlight.

But he was gone.

Ava felt a surge of paranoia as she glanced around the rest of the parking lot and found that there was no trace of the man. No cars in the parking lot were missing, which led Ava to believe that the man was still walking around on the property.

Ava thought about saying something but instead decided to just make sure the apartment door was locked. Uncle Matthew didn't live in the best part of town, but there had never been any break-ins at the apartment complex. Having a police detective living there probably helped.

"Dinner's ready," Uncle Matthew yelled from the kitchen.

Ava walked over to the counter where a bowl of cereal and a spoon sat in front of her. Uncle Matthew sat next to her, slurping up his Rice Krispies.

The two ate in silence for a couple minutes. Uncle Matthew set down his bowl after drinking the remaining milk from his cereal.

"How is your latest book coming along? Are you still working on that story you were telling me about?"

Uncle Matthew was always supportive of Ava's writing. The fact that he was a detective was fascinating to her and was the reason she began writing books about crime and mysteries.

"I've…been a little uninspired lately, I haven't worked on anything in a while to be honest."

"Well, I'm sure you'll find your inspiration again, you always do."

Matthew got up from his stool, approached the sink and proceeded to rinse his bowl.

"I wanted to let you know that part of this summer won't be spent like it normally is," he said.

Ava swallowed her bite with a gulp and said, "What do you mean?"

Uncle Matthew placed his bowl in the sink and turned around to face Ava.

"You know I rarely go on cases that involve travel, so when I do, they have to be something special, right?"

Ava nodded.

"Well, I was offered a case about a week ago from a department in another town, and I chose to take the case," Uncle Matthew said rubbing his neck sheepishly.

"That's great! I mean I know you don't go away on many cases, so this must be particularly important," Ava said grinning, "When do you have to go?"

"That's the thing, Ava," Uncle Matthew sighed, "I leave tomorrow morning."

Ava felt her smile fade.

"Oh," she said looking down at her cereal.

"I know this is very sudden and I'm so sorry for waiting until the day before to tell you; I was afraid that if I told you before you arrived you wouldn't come home for the summer. I rarely get to see you, which is why I found a solution to this predicament," Uncle Matthew said with a growing smile on his face.

"What?" Ava asked slowly taking another bite.

"You…can accompany me on the case!" Uncle Matthew gushed.

Ava almost choked on her food.

"What? How?"

"It's not a big deal," Uncle Matthew said, "the guys at the police station where we're going have agreed to it, including Chief Sean. Everyone at that department is really friendly," Uncle Matthew said, "It would have to be unofficial of course, but it would be a great experience for you. We can spend time together and, hell, maybe it'll give you some ideas for your new book! They're even going to pay for an extra room at the hotel there for you. It's nothing fancy but it's nice enough. It even has a pool!"

"I would love to go!" Ava cheered, "But aren't these cases, like, serious? I mean, I'd probably be a bother."

"Not at all! Of course, this *is* a serious case and there is a limit to what information you'd be able to know… not that I don't trust you, but some aspects of the case might be confidential. However, you could come with me to some of the meetings…and we can always have lunch and dinner together!"

Hearing her uncle talk excitedly about the upcoming case made her happy, and without another thought, she agreed to come with him.

"Wait, really?" Uncle Matthew flashed a giddy smile. "I thought there would be more persuasion involved."

"No! I would love to come with you," Ava said smiling.

"Wow, this is great! We'll have so much fun, I promise."

"We will,"

Uncle Matthew checked his Casio calculator watch.

"Oh, it's ten fifteen. We should go to bed."

Ava grabbed her bowl and washed it out before placing it in the sink.

"You don't even need to unpack, just bring your suitcase as it is. We need to get on the road at six," Uncle Matthew said while turning off the lights in the living room, "then we can discuss the case on the ride over."

"What does the case involve?" Ava asked as she flipped off the lights from the kitchen.

Matthew slowly turned to her.

"Murder," he whispered as if someone was eavesdropping.

"Really?" Ava was shocked.

"Possibly. I'll tell you more in the morning," he said, "I'm gonna get ready for bed. Goodnight, Ava. I'm so glad you're back."

Ava noticed that the moon was shining through the window as the clouds began to clear out of the night sky.

"The moon sure is bright," she said.

"Yep," said Matthew, "It's a blood moon in a couple of days. Hopefully, it'll be clear enough to where we can see it."

"What exactly is a blood moon again?"

"It's a total lunar eclipse that only happens every few years or so. The moon goes blood red for a while, it's pretty neat."

"That's cool," Ava said recalling a similar conversation, but she was too tired to even try to remember it.

"'Night, Uncle Matthew," she said with a yawn.
She watched as he walked into his bedroom and closed the door behind him. Ava grabbed her suitcase and ambled to her bedroom.

The sign on the door to her bedroom read:

Ava's Room: Keep Out!

She wrote it herself in her old middle school handwriting. She smiled as she opened the door.

The room hadn't changed since she was thirteen, and it looked a lot like her room in her old house when her parents were alive. Posters of Ralph Macchio and *The Smiths* filled her walls.

Embroidered poppies covered her bedsheets, blankets, and pillowcases. Her dresser and desk's white paint was chipped on the corners, and polaroid pictures of her and her friends were taped to the wall above her bed. The ceiling was covered with glow-in-the-dark stars that barely glowed anymore, but served as faint nightlights when she turned off the overhead light.

Ava set her suitcase on her bed and took out her sleepwear. Then she went to her desk and took off her necklace. The purple stone seemed to glow brighter than the moonbeams that were sneaking into her bedroom window. After she changed into her pajamas and brushed her teeth with the half empty tube of Aim toothpaste left in the bathroom, she climbed into bed. Ava watched her ceiling stars' glow slowly fade as she gradually drifted off to sleep without another thought.

At an abandoned warehouse. a tall man in a dark, hooded cloak made his way into a large room filled with old wooden crates. A few lights hung from the ceiling which flickered occasionally creating enough light to see to move around. Cobwebs lingered in every corner and crevice. Inside that room, a group of men and women dressed in dark, hooded robes surrounded a fragile looking woman who sat in a wheelchair. The man shut the door behind him and made his way through the crowd as they parted to form a path to the frail old woman.

He took off his black hood and knelt before her.

"Did you see the girl?" the wheelchaired woman asked in a low, raspy voice.

"Yes, I did, ma'am," the man said.

Gasps came from the crowd as they began to circle around once again.

"And was she wearing it?"

“I believe so.”

“Wonderful,” the fragile woman said smiling, “this will all be over very soon.”

The crowd broke out into a cheer as the two smiled at each other.

The old warehouse stood in an overgrown forest in a small town.

A town named Parkfield.

Chapter Two

The next day was bright and cheerful, and so was Uncle Matthew who had been up since four packing and singing *Don't Stop Believing* but very offkey.

Ava woke up to his warbling, rubbed her eyes and checked the time on the alarm clock next to her: 5:23 AM. She trudged out of her room squinting her eyes, trying to adjust to the searing morning light from the windows.

Uncle Matthew was in the kitchen frying eggs. He wore a white polo shirt and another pair of khaki cargo pants. The radio that sat on the small counter was talking about the weather.

"The rain has moved out of our area and it's going to be a beautiful day with highs of eighty-three and lows of seventy-two..."

"Good morning, Uncle Matthew," Ava said as she sat on one of the stools at the counter.

"Good morning!" he said in a chipper voice. He grabbed two plates from the cabinet and placed the fried eggs on them before turning around and handing a plate to Ava.

"I made your favorite type of eggs!" He grinned an incredibly happy grin.

"Thank you!" Ava rubbed her eyes before retrieving the plate and grabbing silverware from one of the drawers.

Uncle Matthew seated himself next to her and turned down the radio.

"So," Uncle Matthew said as he took a bite, "I finished packing, whenever we finish eating and you get ready, we can leave."

Ava nodded and began to eat.

After a few bites she asked, "Can you tell me about this case now?"

Uncle Matthew smiled.

"Sure, listen to this," he leaned in close as if it were a secret, "About a week ago, a group of tourists were hiking through the mountains of this small town where we're going. They discovered the body of a man who seemed to have fallen off a cliff behind where his body was found. However, the local police there believe it was a murder."

"Why do they think it was a murder? Maybe he committed suicide. Or he could have just been hiking and fallen," she said.

"They ran an autopsy a couple days ago and determined signs of strangulation. And at the top of the cliff where he fell, there was evidence of a struggle…so he may have been pushed or thrown off."

"Wow," Ava said as she ate another bite of her eggs, "that is suspicious."

"Truly. And get this, in a backpack on his person he had several sticks of dynamite and a detonator."

"Dynamite? Well, I guess he wasn't just hiking."

"This may be the most interesting case I've ever been on. This is a ginormous deal."

Matthew checked his watch and immediately picked up his plate.

"Is it time to go?" Ava climbed off of her stool and grabbed her plate.

"Yes. I'll take care of the dishes. Go on and grab your suitcase. Oh, and please brush your teeth," he said while scrubbing off his plate before he placed it in the dishwasher.

"Sure," Ava said as she trekked to her bedroom where she closed her suitcase and got ready.

Before walking out of her room, she turned to her desk and noticed the necklace her father had given her.

"Ava! We need to go!" Uncle Matthew exclaimed from the kitchen.

"Coming!" Ava snatched the necklace, swiftly clipped it around her neck and tucked it into her shirt before running out of her room. Uncle Matthew was putting his gun in his holster when she passed by him. He never was a big fan of guns and said he only drew it when he absolutely had to, but it was part of his job. They left the apartment and headed down the hallway.

As they exited the elevator into the apartment lobby, Debra, sitting at her desk, caught sight of Matthew and Ava leaving.

"What are you grinning about, Matthew?" the old woman snarked. She looked grumpier than the day before which made Ava shiver.

"My niece and I are going out of town on a case!" Uncle Matthew trilled.

"Oh, right. I almost forgot. You're the hotshot detective," Debra said rolling her eyes, "Good luck with all of that."

Ava walked behind her uncle, clutching the handle on her suitcase.

"Thank you!" Uncle Matthew said grinning as they both exited the building.

The old woman scoffed and pushed her glasses up her nose, grabbed the gossip magazine off her desk and continued to read.

The sky was a pretty blue and the blaring sun dominated the sky. The two walked through the parking lot to Uncle Matthew's little white car. Her uncle excitedly opened the trunk and placed both suitcases inside. He threw their extra bags in the back seat before they both climbed into the car.

When they were buckled in, Uncle Matthew rummaged through his briefcase and pulled out a large envelope.

"This is all the information that the police department know about the man so far," he said as he handed Ava the letter, "It's not much, but it's something."

She opened the flap to the envelope and pulled out a sheet of paper. As Matthew drove out of the parking lot, Ava began to read:

The victim's name was Henry Van Scott, a lifelong local resident. Locals around town knew Mr. Van Scott, but weren't closely acquainted with him, saying that he was quiet and kept to himself. Although unacquainted with most residents in the town, he had one close friend—Abraham Solomon who owns a second-hand shop called SeEkS in town. Abraham refused to tell us anything that would help with the case.

"So, I'm guessing you're going to question Abraham Solomon?" Ava placed the paper back into the envelope.

"Yes, and you're coming with me as my assistant," he said joyfully.

Ava smiled and placed the envelope back into his briefcase as Uncle Matthew pulled onto a busy highway.

The girl exchanged her uncle's briefcase for her backpack and placed it onto her lap. She rifled through the books inside until she found the true crime book that had a bookmark in it. She pulled it out, zipped up her backpack and threw her bag back into the backseat.

"Are you sure you don't want me to drive?" Ava asked.

"I'm sure. You can read."

Uncle Matthew stared at the road in front of him and drove at a steady pace.

She opened her book at the bookmark and began reading.

The sky began to fill with various shades of grey, but sunbeams managed to escape the clutch of the altostratus clouds to provide plenty of reading light. Inside the car, it felt humid. A storm was brewing.

After about a half-hour of reading, Ava gradually grew tired and set her book down. She leaned her seat back and fell asleep in a few short moments.

She opened her eyes quickly and found herself in a bed. The room was dark, and she was unable to identify anything other than the white sheets that she rested under. A small window appeared in the distance with soft blue curtains. Tree branches spread outside the window, and within a moment, a dove appeared on one of the branches. The small bird looked around, taking in its surroundings, when its gaze fell on Ava's. The dove watched Ava, and in one swift movement, it flew away.

"Wait!" she yelled at the bird. Tears began to stream out of her eyes. "Come back! Please!"

"Ava?" a familiar voice echoed back from inside the room. It sounded like her mother's voice.

Suddenly, the bed somehow opened up into a hole and Ava found herself plunging into complete darkness and nothingness. The smell of lavender tea swept into her nose and a sense of calm nostalgia came over her. She continued to fall for what felt like hours, tears occasionally escaping from her eyes. It was a silent fall, it almost seemed peaceful.

Ava woke up with a jolt. As she opened her eyes, rain was pelting the roof of Uncle Matthew's car as the windshield wipers swiftly moved side to side. The road was no longer a highway, it was more of a two-lane backroad.

"Hey sleepyhead," Uncle Matthew said.

"Hey," Ava yawned and rubbed her eyes, "are we almost there?"

"As a matter of fact, yes. Did you have a bad dream?"

"I'm not sure," Ava said as she gazed out the window. Trees and mountainous fields were the only things surrounding them.

Ava felt a sinking feeling take over her. Uncle Matthew drove up a hill onto a mountain road. The place felt oddly familiar to Ava as they passed a sign welcoming them to their destination.

"Parkfield…" Ava mumbled. She *knew* that name.

Uncle Matthew continued along the rain-soaked mountain road. To the car's left was guard rail to prevent cars from toppling off of the cliff and to their right was a high mountain wall next to the road.

"Uncle Matthew, why does this place seem so familiar?" Ava inquired.

Matthew sighed, "This is…the highway where your parents died."

Ava felt her heart drop as the realization of the location came over her.

"What…*what*?!" Ava breathed.

"I was going to tell you…I…just didn't know how."

"Why didn't you tell me before now?" she raised her voice angrily.

"I'm sorry, Ava," Matthew whimpered.

He continued to drive facing forward and not even glancing at Ava. She could hear the pain in his voice.

"I need this case. I need the money. And I really wanted you here with me. My brother's death haunts me too...have you ever thought about how hard this has been on me?"

Ava watched her uncle in a silence that made the rain sound louder as it pelted the car. A sun ray poked out from the clouds and beamed itself to the ground below.

In a few moments, the rain dissipated and the clouds began to clear away.

"I am sorry," Uncle Matthew began. "I don't get asked to go on cases much anymore, and although this is probably the worst location, I decided to be professional about it and accept it. I understand that you're upset, but I hoped seeing this highway after all this time, we could both try moving forward…moving on."

Ava watched tears form in her uncle's eyes, and she couldn't help but feel sorry for him.

"I understand," she said after another minute of silence.

"Thank you," he sighed.

She watched as he quickly wiped a tear that slid down his cheek and exhaled. They continued traveling along the wet, mountain road.

After a few minutes, their car passed by what looked to be a crime scene on the mountain. Police tape hung around a part of the guard rail and attached to two trees on the other side which created a triangular border. Two police cars were parked next to it and a group of people in uniform gathered around the police tape. They seemed to be inspecting every small thing around it.

"I take it that's where Henry died," Ava said as she turned in her seat to view the scene once more before it disappeared in the distance.

"I believe so," Matthew stated.

"I suppose they're still looking for obvious clues, right?"

"Very true. We have no real leads as of now. And all this rain I'm sure isn't helping that search."

"What about the shop owner at that junk store?" Ava inquired, "Abraham…he might be of some help."

"Perhaps. He probably knew Henry Van Scott the best," Uncle Matthew said.

As Matthew continued driving, Ava began to see buildings in the distance.

"They already tried speaking to Abraham but said that he didn't reveal much at all. He's an interesting character and not a very talkative person. That's one of the reasons they want me on this case, I'm pretty good with interrogations."

"I know you are," Ava said proudly.

As Matthew continued driving, small buildings appeared on each side of the road bordered by empty sidewalks. Although the town was in its own way pretty, the deserted streets made Ava feel uneasy.

"Where is everyone?" she asked.

"Beats me," Matthew answered.

"So, where are we going first?"

"We're going to check into our motel and then bring you to the station where you can meet everyone who's working on the case," Uncle Matthew said grinning, "It's gonna be a blast."

Ava stared out of her window smiling. They passed a row of houses all lined up neatly with a large forest sprawling through each of their backyards. The forest looked dark and intimidating. Ava didn't dare to look at it for too long.

They continued to drive down the empty road. The town of Parkfield seemed small and uneventful, not a place where many tourists would like to visit. The sun perched high above, scaring off whatever cloud dared to steal its property.

Ava has yet to figure out why her parents, her father especially, wanted to visit this town. The more she looked the more she wondered what was so important about Parkfield.

A small parking lot with an old sign that read *Field Inn Motel* could be spotted in the distance with a motel beside it that seemed even smaller. Trees surrounded the quaint, one-story building which was long and full of windows.

They pulled into the parking lot of the Field Inn Motel, which was surprisingly filled with cars. Only two spaces were left vacant, Uncle Matthew pulled into one of them and parked.

"We're here!" he exclaimed.

"I'm glad," Ava said as she opened the car door and started to stretch, "My legs fell asleep."

Uncle Matthew opened the trunk and grabbed their luggage while Ava dug in the backseat for her backpack and her uncle's briefcase.

The two ambled inside the lobby and continued to the front desk where a man stood smiling.

"Welcome to The Field Inn! My name is Marty, how can I help you?"

The man wore a white, buttoned up shirt and his brown hair was slicked back with way too much gel.

"Hi. I'm Matthew Sinclair and this is my niece, Ava Sinclair. We have reservations."

"Indeed, you do!" Marty agreed, "Both of you please sign in on the register in front of you then I can get you both your room keys."

Uncle Matthew grabbed a pen from a cup filled with writing utensils next to the ledger and signed his name, then stepped aside so that Ava could sign hers.

"I'm guessing you two are here for the 'top secret' case in town," the man behind the desk said.

"How did you know about that?" Uncle Matthew asked.

"Oh, forgive me, I didn't mean to overstep my bounds. I know the police department is paying for your rooms and, well, everyone here knows about the case. It's the talk of the town." he replied with a grin on his face, "Old Henry, falling off that cliff with a backpack full of dynamite! You see, gossip spreads like wildfire in this town."

"Oh, I see," Uncle Matthew looked as if he was thinking for a moment, then got into detective mode and continued, "Did you know Henry Van Scott?"

"A little. Good guy. Always kept to himself, though. We in the community all tried becoming friends with him at some point, but he always kinda pushed us away," Marty said.

"So, you don't know why he would have been up on that cliff with a pack full of dynamite."

"No idea, maybe he just went crazy…I hope you can get to the bottom of it! Oh, let me get your keys."

He turned away from Ava and Matthew as he grabbed two keys that sat side by side on two hooks on the wall and turned back around to hand them over.

"Your rooms are down the hall about halfway down. Have a nice stay!"

"Thank you," said Uncle Matthew.

Before walking away, Ava noticed Marty staring at her, but she didn't think too much of it. She followed her uncle down the hall.

The tag on Ava's key read '13', while her uncle's key read '14.'

"Let me take lucky number thirteen, you get fourteen," Uncle Matthew said.

Light barely glowed in the long hallway. Between each door, an odd painting was nailed to the wall. One had a strange clown looking as if it were piercing into Ava's soul, while another one was simply a barn that stood alone on a grassy field with sunflowers along the bottom. The paintings gave Ava a strange vibe but she ignored it and continued down the hall.

Nine… ten… eleven… she counted in her head.

"Fourteen." she said aloud.

The wooden door looked old and appeared to have been stained a dark brown color many times. Bold, slightly crooked numbers that made '14' had been nailed onto the door. Ava turned the key and opened up her room.

"Be ready in about ten minutes, all right?" Uncle Matthew asked from the doorway next to hers as he entered his room.

Ava smiled and nodded as she closed and locked the door behind her.

After their voices and footsteps were no longer audible, Marty at the front desk picked up the phone and dialed a number. A smirk sprawled across his face.

"She just checked in. Her and her uncle," Marty informed the person on the other line, "and she's going to be assisting with the case, just like you had hoped."

Chapter Three

Ava's room was small but cozy. A queen-sized bed sat against a wall with nightstands on either side. Pink flowered wallpaper walls surrounded her as if she was being swallowed by tacky garden. She placed her clothes in the dresser by the window then stored her suitcase in a small closet by her bed. A surprisingly healthy small potted plant rested on top of the dresser; its leaves radiating beauty. In her small bathroom, she placed her bag of bathroom necessities under the sink as she nodded in the mirror with a sense of achievement. When she had finished unpacking, she turned off the lights to her hotel room and opened the door to leave.

Arriving at the lobby, she noticed Uncle Matthew sitting on one of the couches near a brick fireplace. He checked his watch impatiently and looked over at a couple who were at the front desk talking to Marty. They were busy complaining about how the pool out back didn't match what the pool looked like in the hotel's brochure.

"There you are!" Uncle Matthew said as he saw Ava approaching him.

"Sorry if I took too long," Ava said.

"You didn't! I'm just excited to see my friends from the police department. I haven't seen them in so long," Uncle Matthew said eagerly, "Let's go!"

On the way, Uncle Matthew began filling Ava in on the many adventures he had with his fellow coworkers on previous cases. The cases were not nearly as exciting as this one, so the stories were pretty boring. Ava made sure to show excitement and interest while her uncle talked.

They soon reached the town once more and drove past the tiny, sun-bleached buildings. A few people were now walking on the streets wearing dull colors; grays, browns and blacks. They all had solemn faces as they trudged to where ever their destinations were.

"What a sad looking town," Ava sighed as she gazed out the window.

"Truly," Uncle Matthew said. "Now as I was saying, Robert and I were laughing hysterically when we saw Eddie, we call him Sleepy because he used to fall asleep at his desk all the time! We did stop calling him that once he was diagnosed with narcolepsy…anyways, wait, uh, what was I saying?"

They arrived at the police station a few minutes later. The brown-bricked building was small with several police and regular cars in the parking lot. Worn tires and faded paint from the vehicles stared dully at Ava, except for a motorcycle parked in the very last parking space which caught Ava's attention. It had a bright red stripe on both sides of its black frame. Though it seemed like an older, vintage model, it appeared vibrant and exciting. Breathtaking, even.

"That's Chief Sean's motorcycle," Uncle Matthew stated as he found a parking spot, "It's his pride and joy."

Ava chuckled at his comment.

She noticed a few people in uniforms enter the station lock eyes with her for a moment. Ava was taken aback, but quickly lost interest in their gaze as soon as Uncle Matthew continued speaking.

"So, I'll introduce you to my coworkers and afterwards let you hang out a little. Unfortunately, I have a meeting with some of the higherups and you can't be in there for that. The meeting will most likely take twenty minutes or so."

Ava nodded her head and opened her car door to get out.

She followed her uncle into the building. They were immediately greeted by a bearded man who looked to be in his fifties.

"Is that who I think it is?" the man practically screamed at Uncle Matthew.

"Jacob!" Uncle Matthew laughed. The incredibly happy man pulled Uncle Matthew into what closely resembled a bear hug. "I haven't seen you in, like, a year or so!"

"I missed you, bud!" Jacob said as he released Uncle Matthew from his embrace and revealed a genuine smile.

"Same here!" Uncle Matthew turned to Ava, who stood awkwardly behind him. Jacob's eyes followed Uncle Matthew's as he looked at her.

"Don't tell me…" Jacob said as he walked over to stand next to Ava, "Is this the famous Ava Sinclair?"

"Guilty," Ava said with a sheepish smile.

"Sergeant Jacob, this is my niece, Ava."

"Wow!" Jacob exclaimed, "Matthew has told me *so* much about you. You're almost a celebrity around here!"

"I am?" Ava said as she looked at her uncle who simply smiled and shrugged.

"Yes, you are!" Jacob continued, "I know you go to Harvard, and you are super smart, and, uh," he thought for a moment, "and you write stories, correct?"

"Yes, I suppose that describes me pretty well," Ava said.

"We would love to catch up, Jacob," Uncle Matthew started, "but I have a meeting with Sean and the guys."

"Ooh, Sean…he's in a mood today. Good luck with all of that," Jacob said as if he were trying to frighten Uncle Matthew, "He's a pretty scary one, wouldn't you say?"

"Sometimes I suppose, but he's a good guy," Uncle Matthew uttered.

"Sean with the motorcycle?" Ava asked her uncle.

"Yes, he's the chief here." Uncle Matthew said, "and he's very serious about his job."

"He hates people who slack off," Jacob added.

"Like you," Uncle Matthew said with a smile at Jacob who rolled his eyes in return.

"He doesn't yell at me as much anymore, maybe once or twice a week," Jacob countered.

Ava and Uncle Matthew chuckled.

"Well, I shouldn't keep the chief waiting. See you later, Jacob."

"Bye guys!" Jacob said with a wave.

Ava slightly smiled at her uncle's friend before running after Uncle Matthew who was already making his way down a white hallway.

"So, I'm not exactly sure where the meeting room is, but I do know that there is a break room in this hallway," he told Ava as they walked, "You can stay in there. I shouldn't be too long."

They passed by a few metal, industrial-looking doors each with a small window looking into each room. Uncle Matthew abruptly stopped in his tracks when he heard voices coming from one of the rooms and peeked through the window.

"I'm pretty sure this is it," Matthew said as he knocked on the door in front of him.

"Come in," someone yelled from inside.

Uncle Matthew opened the door and entered with Ava close behind.

The room was small, with light grey walls and dark grey tiled floors. A large, dark, round meeting table sat in the center of the room with every chair taken except one. All of the men looked to be in their late forties or early fifties except for one who looked to be in his early thirties. He had dark black hair that was cut in a clean manner and was drinking what seemed to be black coffee from a teacup. His head was down as he intently went over some paperwork. He didn't even attempt to move his eyes toward the entrance where Matthew and Ava stood, while everyone else's heads shot up in their direction acknowledging the two with warm smiles. Ava noticed the younger-looking man drank from his teacup in a strange way. Instead of holding the cup by the handle, he grasped the entire top of the rim.

"Matthew! How wonderful to see you!" one of the older men said from his seat. Others around the table nodded in agreement.

"You too, Aaron!" Matthew exclaimed.

"Who's the girl?" the younger man asked. His tone almost sounded forceful and somewhat rude.

"Oh, uh, this is my niece, Ava," Matthew said somewhat nervously.

"Tch," was all the man said as he looked at Ava.

"Chief Sean, sir, I thought you gave permission for her to be here," said Uncle Matthew.

So, this is the chief, Ava thought. Although handsome, well-groomed and younger than the rest of the police force, he seemed rather intimidating like Sergeant Jacob said. His grey eyes pierced into Ava's, and she felt herself almost jump. He *was* quite intimidating.

"I did, I suppose," he said without expression, and looked away from Ava immediately after speaking, "she can't be in here for this meeting."

"Oh, of course not. But thanks again for letting me bring her along, sir," Uncle Matthew responded sincerely.

"I heard you go to Harvard," one of the other men commented to Ava.

"Yes, I do."

"Hm. I had a friend who went there," the man said, "He died."

The room went completely silent until the man laughed at his own comment. Everyone stared in confusion.

"Alright," another man said, "we should begin."

"Okay," Uncle Matthew turned to Ava, "the break room is two doors down, you'll find it."

Ava nodded.

"It would be best if you didn't interrupt us," the chief stated plainly. He began writing something on the paper in front of him, Ava noticed how neat his handwriting was.

"Yes sir," she mumbled.

"I'll get you when we're done," Uncle Matthew said smiling at her.

"Okay." Ava turned to face the men. "It was nice meeting all of you."

The men nodded and said goodbye, except for the chief who simply continued to sip his coffee.

Ava left the room and slowly closed the door behind her. She could hear murmurs from inside the room as they started their meeting.

She looked around the empty hallway until she found the break room. She opened the door to find another small room. It was painted a dark brown color, and once again grey tile covered the floor. A small T.V. was mounted on the wall and a small kitchen was in the corner next to the television. An old, beat-up orange couch was placed in front of the T.V. allowing a clear view of the screen. The lights were dim but a window at the back wall projected enough light to fill most of the room. Ava plopped herself down on the ugly orange couch and tilted her head up to watch the screen. It was simply the news and it quickly bored her after watching it for a couple minutes. She felt herself growing tired, and as the quiet murmurs from the television grew to silence, she fell asleep.

"Ava?" a voice said softly.

Ava began to stir.

"Ava?" the voice said again.

"Un-Uncle Matthew?" Ava rubbed her eyes before opening them.

But it wasn't Uncle Matthew.

And she was no longer in the break room.

Chapter Four

Ava's vision was quite blurry, and she was unable to open her eyes all the way.

Even with her struggling vision, she was able to locate herself in a familiar looking room. She was once again in a bed, a small window with soft blue curtains faced her from the opposite wall. Branches from a tree outside swayed in the wind.

Murmurs surrounded her, growing louder with every second. Suddenly, someone stood over Ava and flashed a light into her eyes. Once on her left, and once on her right.

Many unidentifiable people surrounded her bed. She tried to say something, anything, but her lips remained shut. It seemed as if she was completely paralyzed so she was unable to do anything.

She woke up to the sound of a door opening and the low sounds of reporters muttering on the T.V. Ava rubbed her eyes and realized that she was back in the police station's breakroom. She shrugged off her dream and was thankful that she was now in a familiar place.

Suddenly, somebody plopped down next to her on the couch. Ava froze when she saw it was the chief.

Remote in one hand and his coffee in the other, he flipped through channels. Abrupt yelling, talking and commercial jingles filled the empty room from the different stations. Finally, he stopped on the same news broadcast that was playing when Ava first walked in.

"There's never anything good on," he said to himself.

He continued to watch the screen with a bored expression, while Ava watched him with curiosity.

The first thing she noticed again was his brilliantly pale, grey eyes. She had never met anyone with such breathtaking eyes.

He sat in a still position, ignoring her presence entirely. When he did move, it was to take another sip of his almost-empty coffee cup. She couldn't help but feel drawn to him, though he was older and apparently a pain in the ass to be around.

"Do you need something?" he asked while still glued to the television.

"Sorry, uh, no. I'm fine. Umm, is… your meeting done already?" Ava asked awkwardly.

"Not yet, but I don't have to be there, it's my choice," he replied.

"Oh," Ava looked at her hands, fumbling her thumbs over each other.

"Why are you here?" he asked as he finally looked at her. She felt her heart skip a beat as both of his eyes zeroed in on hers. Ava quickly averted her eyes down to her hands.

"Oh, uh, I stay with my uncle over the summer, he's my guardian, and he had this case, so he brought me with him," Ava mumbled.

A silence fell. She finally had the courage to look up to see why Sean hadn't replied. He was again watching T.V. and sipping his coffee.

Ouch, Ava thought, *didn't even respond.*

"Aren't you the girl whose parents died in that car crash? Pretty sure your uncle has talked about it once or twice," Sean said blatantly.

"Oh, uh, yeah. That's me," Ava sighed and looked at her hands again.

"That's a shame. So…that was eight years ago, right? How old were you then?" he inquired as he looked at her again.

"It was six years ago, I was thirteen," Ava mumbled. She did not like the topic they were discussing.

"You're nineteen?" Sean asked her.

She nodded.

"Huh, you don't look nineteen."

He turned back to face the TV, but his lips perked into a noticeable smirk.

They sat in silence again, the news ended and another commercial started. A girl was pitching a brand-new type of mattress, apparently wonderful for a restful sleep. As if that wasn't the whole point of owning a mattress in the first place.

"This girl annoys me," Sean said as he switched the channel to a random movie.

Ava chuckled a little.

Sean glanced at Ava, a smile formed on his lips, which disappeared quickly.

Then, suddenly, the door to the breakroom opened as Uncle Matthew walked in.

Ava turned around and grinned at her uncle.

"The meeting's over?" she asked.

"It sure is," her uncle said, "Chief, I'm surprised you left early, you missed a great meeting wrap-up."

"Tch, I go to plenty of meetings and I was bored. If I miss anything important, I'll get briefed later," Chief Sean said not even turning to look at Uncle Matthew.

Her uncle playfully rolled his eyes at him, which made Ava laugh.

"Well, we should get going. Want to go eat at that diner, Ava?" Uncle Matthew asked.

"Sure!" Ava said rising up from the couch.

She and Matthew walked out of the room. Ava hesitated for a moment but turned back to face Sean.

"Nice to meet you, I'll see you later, I'm sure."

"See ya," Chief Sean said in a very low voice never taking his eyes off the T.V.

The sun began to sink behind the hills on the outskirts of town as they drove. After a little while, they saw the sign for Ruby's Diner in the pale orange sunlight.

"Here we are!" Uncle Matthew said as he pulled into parking lot and got out of the car.

When Ava got out, she noticed the diner was part of a row of buildings that formed a plaza. A doctor's office stood at one end and a liquor store on the other.

Across the street was *SeEkS,* the thrift store where Abraham worked.

"Look, there's *SeEkS!*" exclaimed Ava noticing how dark it was inside, "I guess it's not open right now."

"I'm sure Mr. Abraham keeps weird hours, at least we know right where it is. We'll go by there tomorrow," Matthew said.

As they walked inside the diner, Ava asked, "Is this supposed to be a pretty good place to eat?"

"Yeah. Jacob told me the food here is good and that their milkshakes are excellent!"

When they walked in, they saw lots of empty tables and booths. The floor was made of red and white checkered tiles and there was a bar at the end of the diner with several tall stools in front of it. There was only one customer sitting at a table drinking a milkshake. A young man eagerly greeted them from behind the counter.

"Welcome to Ruby's Diner! You two have a seat anywhere you like!"

They both sat in a red booth that seemed quite worn but fit the stereotypical diner vibe quite nicely. The placemats were the menus and there was even a jukebox that played old 45 records. The waiter walked over to their table.

"Howdy! You folks from out of town, ain't ya?"

"Not too far from here," said Matthew.

"Well, welcome to Parkfield, where are y'all stayin'?"

"The Field Inn Motel."

"Oooh, fancy! Well, I hope you enjoy your stay, what can I get for ya?"

"Could I get the cheeseburger with ketchup and mustard, fries, and a vanilla milkshake?" Ava asked.

"Sure! And for you?" He looked at Uncle Matthew.

"I'll have the salad with ranch dressing."

"What to drink?"

"Water, please."

"Okay, great! I will get those right out!"

The waiter suddenly noticed Ava's necklace which was showing outside of the top she changed into at the motel.

"What a…beautiful necklace you're wearing, ma'am," he said glaringly.

"Thanks…my father gave it to me," Ava said as she brushed her fingertips against the stone.

After a few more seconds, the waiter turned and headed to the kitchen to get their order placed.

Weird, Ava thought.

"So, how was your 'first day'?" Uncle Matthew asked.

"Well, uneventful I guess."

"True, a lot of detective work is boring, it's part of the job."

"I'm pretty tired, though."

Uncle Matthew checked his watch. "Well, we did skip lunch, I bet you're starving. Some food will help."

"Yes, you're probably right," Ava sighed, "What time do we have to wake up tomorrow?"

"Seven thirty am, *sharp*."

"Okay."

After some time, the waiter walked out with a tray of food and set it down on their table.

"A cheeseburger with fries and a salad with ranch dressing," he said as he placed the plates in front of Ava and Uncle Matthew, "and your drinks."

"Thank you!" Ava smiled.

"Thanks, I can take the check now as well," Uncle Matthew said.

"Sure thing, here ya go!" The waiter smiled, put the ticket on their table and walked back into the kitchen.

After a little while, Ava and Uncle Matthew finished their meals.

"I'm ready," said Ava.

"Me too. Let's go. We'll peek into *SeEkS*, I'm curious to see what it looks like in there."

Uncle Matthew set money down on the table with the check under it as they headed out.

"Thanks for coming in!" yelled the waiter.

"Thank you, it was very good!" Ava said as they both walked out the door. The waiter's smile faded into a scowl as he watched them walk over to *SeEkS*. The man who was drinking the shake got up from his seat to watch Matthew and Ava as well.

"Sit down, Harry, don't let them see you," the waiter said as he picked up the phone, dialed a number and after a couple of rings, began talking with someone.

"I saw it with my own eyes…she has it," he whispered.

Ava and Matthew approached the closed thrift store. In the window they could see all sorts of things from old clothes to toys to scented candles to mounted animal heads on the sage green walls. A handwritten sign on the counter said:

Half off all voodoo dolls.

Along the inside of the window sill that they were looking through lay several dead stink bugs.

"Hmmm…interesting place," said Uncle Matthew, "guess we'll have to hit this again in the morning. Let's get back to the motel now." They both got back in the car and pulled out of the parking lot.

"Actually, do you mind if I drop you off back at the motel? I need to go back to the police station and grab some more paperwork," Uncle Matthew said.

"Oh, that's fine," Ava said.

When they got to the Field Inn, Ava climbed out of the car.

"I'll be back. Got your key?" Matthew asked.

"Yep, see you soon!"

Uncle Matthew smiled and drove away.

Ava got back inside her room, locked the door and changed into her pajamas. She took off her necklace and placed it on the dresser before turning on the T.V. After lying in bed flipping through several uninteresting channels for about half an hour, she heard a knock at her door.

She slowly crept up to the peep hole in her door to see who was outside of her room. In the same moment that she saw it was Uncle Matthew, he knocked once more and sent her jumping backward with a jolt.

"Ava, it's me."

Ava unlocked and opened the door.

"You scared me! Did you get what you needed?"

"Yep, I'll go over it in the morning. Let's get some sleep, been a long day."

"I agree. Hey, would it be all right if you dropped me off at *SeEkS* tomorrow? I won't 'question the person of interest' or anything, just look around and maybe find something cool for my dorm room. I could even go back to Ruby's Diner for breakfast."

"Umm, I guess that will be fine," he replied, "Well, goodnight,"

"'Night."

Ava closed and locked her door, flipped off the lights to her room and climbed into bed, covering herself with the heavy white sheets and blankets. Over on the dresser she could see her necklace giving off a low, purple light. As she stared at the soft glow, thoughts about her necklace filled her mind; *Why were people around here so fascinated with it? What significance does it hold?*

She eventually fell asleep, allowing the sounds of crickets from outside to send her off into a cozy and peaceful slumber.

Chapter Five

The next day, Ava woke up planning on enjoying the blue-skied morning as much as possible; apparently yet another storm was blowing in later. She and Matthew headed out from the motel to his car.

She sat in the seat next to Uncle Matthew watching the road in front of them through the windshield. Familiar buildings came into view, she had begun to recognize the layout of this quirky little town.

"So, I'll drop you off at *SeEkS* and pick you up around eleven or so. Plan on being at the diner around then," Uncle Matthew said to Ava as he drove them into town.

"Okay," she replied, "and I'll just explore a little too since I have plenty of time."

"Yes, you do that. Just be careful. If you need me, you have the number to the station. You got some change for the pay phone?"

"I do," she said.

Uncle Matthew pulled into the parking lot near the thrift store. Ava made sure to tuck her necklace into her shirt just in case Abraham or anyone else in this town took an interest in it.

"Well, I'll see you soon, kiddo," Uncle Matthew said.

"Bye!" Ava said as she opened the car door and climbed out.

She watched as her uncle drove away before turning to face *SeEkS*.

A hand painted '*OPEN*' sign stared at Ava from the window, so she opened the door and walked inside.

The store was everything she had expected, if not more. Shrunken heads hung from the ceilings; voodoo dolls and stuffed dead animals along with all sorts of incense holders and candles crowded dusty shelves. A large tank filled with murky water held two strange, not very healthy-looking fish. Several dead bugs lay scattered along the floor. The lights were dim, but the sunlight that filtered into the store through the front windows allowed enough light for Ava to make her way about the aisles.

On one shelf, she noticed small, strangely shaped, dust covered bottles aligned next to each other. Small handwritten labels were taped onto the fronts. *Sneezing Powder, Laughing Powder, Coughing Powder,* and plenty more. Curious and perhaps a little stupidly, Ava picked up the sneezing powder bottle and twisted it open. She peeked inside the small hole and saw the bottle was halfway filled with a strange green looking powder. She accidently inhaled what was in the bottle and quickly found herself sneezing uncontrollably.

"*Hey!* Quiet down out there, will you?" a man yelled from somewhere inside the store.

Attempting to hold in her sneezes, she turned to find where the voice came from. Next to a counter with a register she saw a door leading to some kind of back room. The light was on in there and the shadow of a person was moving around the doorway.

That must be Abraham.

Another sneeze overtook her, but she managed to call out an apology as she resealed the bottle and put it back.

Soon enough she lost the urge to sneeze and continued looking around the odd store. At the very back, a monkey lamp with a shade that looked like a bunch of bananas sat next to a shelf filled with books. She turned on the lamp which thankfully had enough light so she could make out what the book titles were. She turned to the bookshelf and began to scan through the many books which included *Best Ways to Boil a Cat, Potions 101, Tarot Card Reading for Dummies* and *How to Be a Convincing Voodoo Priest*. Some of the titles she saw on the spines of books made her chuckle. Others were in different languages and still others had unrecognizable symbols that made her shudder a little. She was afraid to even touch those books much less read them; they might hold curses that could haunt her.

Finally, she saw a book entitled *Parkview, Massachusetts: A Supernatural History*. Intrigued, she carefully pulled the book from the shelf. It was old, dusty and heavy. It seemed to consist of several hundred pages. She flipped through the mysterious book finding diagrams of what seemed to be the town along with handwritten notes in the margins next to certain pictures. Her inner detective began to pay attention.

Perhaps Abraham had read this and wrote these notes, she thought.

A few more pages in, she saw illustrations of what seemed to be odd looking gemstones similar to the one on her necklace. The illustration was of four different gems, each the same shape and size. Three of the four gems were crossed out by a line with a pen that had the same color ink as the rest of the notes jotted down. Curiosity overtook her, and she placed the book onto the side table where the lamp was bright enough that she could read the page with better lighting.

Handwritten notes were jotted down next to the pictures of the gems, and an origin story began beneath them. Ava started to read from a random section of the page:

...by the year 1671, it was believed that many of them were scattered throughout this community.

Not even one sentence in, Ava heard a strange creaking sound next to her. She turned to look and suddenly jumped back at the sight of an old man staring at her silently. It must be Abraham, a frail-looking man with spindly limbs and graying stubble on his wrinkled face and bizarre mismatched eyes. One was a milky white, the other a dark color. Neither seemed to look directly at her even though he was staring her down.

"H-hello?" Ava's tone was worrisome, afraid that this was a mad man standing next to her.

He looked at her with a bland, blank expression until he finally spoke up.

"Welcome!" he exclaimed; his mouth twisted into a crooked grin, "Are you looking for anything in particular?"

Ava, shocked by his sudden outburst, shook her head and sheepishly said, "I'm just looking around, thank you."

"We're having a sale on all of our voodoo dolls!"

"Yes, I saw the sign."

He then noticed the book Ava was reading and his eyes widened.

"You seem to be quite interested in that book. I've read it many times myself. Care to buy it?" he asked her in a weirdly joyful tone.

"I'm just browsing through it, it's…interesting," Ava said in a more normal tone, still wondering if perhaps the man was bipolar, crazy or just unusual.

"Oh, that's alright! If you need me just holler, my name's Abraham."

The old man sauntered behind the counter and stood behind an ancient cash register.

Ava followed the strange man. She actually did want to buy the book.

"Well, I do have a question actually, how much…"

"Oh! Before I forget, please take a complimentary pen." Abraham placed his calloused hands on a small, transparent box with a small opening on the top. Inside were many identical pens, each with a navy-blue stripe and the name *SeEkS* printed on them.

"Oh, okay," Ava said.

She carefully placed her hand in the box and pulled out the first pen she touched. It felt soft between her fingers as she placed it in her back pocket.

"I bought too many of these things," Abraham hoarsely chuckled, "I'm just trying to get the word out about the shop, and people love free stuff, right?"

"That's right, and thank you! Anyway, I was just going to ask you..."

"About Henry, Henry Van Scott? His death and who was behind it? No, no, sorry, I will not be discussing that," Abraham said as his tone changed from light to dark. The sunlight from outside dimmed at that moment from incoming cloud cover.

Ava was shocked, all she wanted to do was ask about the price of the book. She told Uncle Matthew that she would not be interrogating Abraham, but here he was volunteering information.

"I have a finger on the pulse of this town, I know things that I should take to my grave without telling anyone…and even though I don't know you, I know you're that detective's daughter."

"I'm actually his niece…"

"Whoever, whatever you are," he interrupted, "I know why you're really here and I will tell you right now, you two don't need to go sticking your nose into business that is much bigger than you are." His once happy face turned solemn.

Ava's detective instincts kicked in and whether that was a good idea or not remained to be seen.

"I-I'm sorry, we're just trying to solve the case surrounding his death," Ava said, "Anything you know might help us do that. I know you knew him. Wasn't he your friend? Was he with anyone else that night?"

Abraham looked deep in thought as he glanced at the book Ava was holding. He finally sighed.

"I can help…by giving you information that will point you and the police in the right direction, but I cannot be held responsible for giving this information to you, do you understand?"

"Yes, I do."

"You probably won't believe me anyway, but I see that you gravitated toward that book about this town. That might be some kind of a sign."

"Thank you," Ava said with a slight smile.

"Follow me, and make sure no one is watching."

Ava instinctively looked out the windows to see if anyone was about to enter the store.

Abraham opened the door behind the counter that led to the backroom and Ava cautiously followed.

Inside this room with no windows, boxes were stacked all over. The only source of light was the lightbulb hung by a frayed wire. A desk with scattered papers sat on the opposite wall. Above the desk were a dozen or so pictures of random things around town; the forest, the cliff, and a couple of buildings Ava had never seen before including a warehouse that looked as if it were in the middle of the forest. In the center of this was a picture of what had to be Henry Van Scott. Purple string was strung along the many pictures around thumbtacks that held the pictures in place.

Abraham must be trying to solve the case as well, Ava thought.

"The first thing you should know is that you and your deputies and whatnot have no idea what Henry's death actually meant," Abraham uttered; his voice dark and almost scary.

"Well," Ava said, "You are our best lead right now."

He shrugged.

"Makes sense, I am the only one who knows the circumstances without being part of the group."

"Group…what group?" Ava asked as she stood by the doorway, ready to run if things got *too* weird.

"Before I tell you anything else, close the door," Abraham said.

Ava paused for a moment, but against her better judgement she shut herself in the storeroom with Abraham.

As he stared at his wall collage, Abraham took a deep breath before saying, "I told the police this, but they didn't believe me. Perhaps you will…I've got a feeling about you."

Abraham turned and looked towards Ava.

"Now, the first thing I must ask is…do you believe in witchcraft?"

Chapter Six

"Do I believe in witchcraft? Yes…I think I do," Ava answered.

"Good," Abraham took a deep breath and began to speak, "Back in the 1600's, witches lived and thrived here in Parkfield. Most were not bad or evil witches who caused harm to humankind and they lived among the townspeople and blended in. That is how the coven of witches kept their magic a secret. Religious leaders during that time did not tolerate any form of witchcraft and sought out anyone practicing magic of any kind. Those who were found out through the years were accused and hanged, others were thrown in prison. A few years after the Salem Witch Trials began, a majority of the witches in this town formed an alliance in order to develop ways to practice their witchcraft that would not draw attention to themselves. Surprisingly, most witches were in the higher economic class, and some were even men. They just wanted to live among us without having to worry about being accused and imprisoned, or worse."

Ava couldn't believe that *this* was the beginning of the story about how the murder of Henry Van Scott occurred. It all sounded as if it were a joke, but the serious look on Abraham's face said this was all true.

"The coven formed an alliance and thrived for several years. The persecutions and accusations of witches decreased in Parkfield. Everything was going well until one witch, Esmerelda, became fed up with the limitations put on witches by the alliance. Clearly, all witches were not big on having restrictions put on themselves, but they knew that some things weren't destined to be and compromise was the best way forward. Esmerelda didn't think like that. She had her own ideas and many of them involved dark magic, magic that could jeopardize humans. Instead of continuing to go forth with the coven's alliance, she wanted to form a rebellion and create a plan that would give the witches power and control over the townspeople of Parkfield. So, in 1663, she presented her idea to the rest of the witches, an idea that was quickly shut down. What Esmerelda wanted went against the entire philosophy of what the coven wanted to achieve—which was to simply live among humans without fear of being persecuted. Their approach never involved ruling over mankind with fear and dark magic. Esmerelda didn't budge and insisted, she even threatened her own coven. After a vote, the society of witches banished Esmerelda from the coven and she was not allowed in Parkfield ever again. Esmerelda was outraged and decided what she was going to do…create an entity that the world had never seen before, a dark force that could not only destroy the human population of Parkfield, but the human population of the entire world."

Shocked, Ava stood silently. She was unable to move or speak. Many things puzzled her; *How does this relate to the murder of Henry Van Scott? Are witches real and are there still witches in Parkfield? How does this man know about all of this?*

"I understand you must be drowning in questions at the moment," Abraham said, "but I promise that when I finish telling you the whole story, you'll understand everything."

Ava nodded from across the room. Abraham continued.

"Now, Esmerelda had been known as one of the most powerful witches in New England. The spells needed to create an entity that could rule over all mankind required large amounts of power, which was why Esmerelda wanted the rest of the coven to help. Since they were not on board with her scheme, over time she was able to conjure up enough of her own energy and dark magic to create a creature that could commit powerful acts of brutality.

The monster she created became known as Finis, which means 'end' in Latin. Finis was a creature entirely new to the magical world, formed by a combination of spells Esmerelda was able to cast. No one knows exactly what it looked like. Some say it was like a large demon. Others say it was like a goat-man hybrid. Whatever it looked like, it was formed days before what is now called a blood moon. Supposedly, when the blood moon officially rose in the sky, Finis would reach full strength. News eventually came around to the head four of the coven: Sarah Yorke, Molly Anne, Elizabeth Goode, and Anne Sinclair."

Sinclair. My last name, Ava thought, *is he saying that I'm related to a witch?*

"The four witches tracked down and confronted Esmerelda, demanding that she not go through with her plan; but her power had grown even stronger as a result of creating Finis and she merely ignored them and fled. The heads of the coven had to make a plan in a hurry to subdue and imprison Esmerelda and Finis. If her creation reached full strength under the blood moon, there would be no way they could overpower it and all humanity could potentially be wiped out.

After conferring with the rest of the coven, they came up with a plan. The four witches were able to track down and capture Esmerelda and Finis on the day of the blood moon using several spells that worked together to contain their power. When they were at their weakest, the four coven leaders trapped her and her monster inside a cave within Mount Redlock, you know, that mountain you have to drive by to get down here? Anyway, the witches successfully sealed up the entrance of the cave with a massive boulder. But there was a problem; the spells that they cast to imprison Esmerelda and Finis had to involve the use of four unique gems each made by one of the four witches…gems known as *dooming stones*. The usage of these stones was flawed in that even though they have the power to trap, they also have the power to free as well. It is told that four holes were carved into the boulder, each one supposedly fits each stone exactly.

So that night, under a blood moon, the owners of the dooming stones placed them in those holes almost like keys in keyholes. They recited an incantation and then the chamber was sealed forever along with the evil within. Now listen to this part carefully. It is told if all four of those gems are reunited and placed within the rock under a blood moon by and *only* by the descendants of those who created the gems, the seal would be undone and the evil would be released."

Ava had to take a moment before she could speak.

"What do these gems look like?" she asked thinking of the hidden necklace around her neck, "There were drawings of them in that book but they were just black and white."

"Legend says that one is a mostly clear with a hint of red, another is an orange-yellow color, and another is a dark shade of green. The final one, made by Anne Sinclair, no one knows about. Each is the same size and shape and they are the only ones of their kind, no other gem resembles how they look. It is also said that each has strange white specks inside that give off a faint glow."

Am I wearing the final dooming stone? Ava asked herself.

"Have you been to that part of the mountain? Are there four holes in a rock wall up there?" Ava asked.

"I went up there years ago. There are lots of holes and cracks and divots in that part of the mountain, so somebody would have to figure out which ones go with the stone. Of course, without the stones, no one has been able to try, but I believe the stones are out there, maybe somewhere not far from Parkfield. It's said that they can't be destroyed, and they have been passed down to descendants of the coven to be protected and never fall into the wrong hands. However, people are known to do all sorts of things that they're not supposed to do."

"Now, how does this have to do with the death of Henry Van Scott?" Ava inquired.

Abraham sighed, his face laced with worry and concern. He didn't respond.

"Aren't you going to tell me? I thought you said that at the end of your story, I would understand everything. I don't."

"You now understand everything you need to understand. Look."

He took a deep breath.

"Parkfield has been built upon secrets since 1663 and some secrets are best kept hidden. It doesn't matter if you believe or not, the truth about Henry's death couldn't be understood by a sane person."

Ava attempted to speak but was cut off by Abraham.

"There are bad people in this town, and it's best you leave before they decide that you and your detective uncle are getting too close to the truth."

Ava shivered. She felt as if she were the main character in a horror movie.

"Heed my warning, this town isn't safe. You still have a shot at escaping. If I were you, I'd run far away from this town and never return. Now I need to get back to the front desk before anyone comes in."

Abraham headed to the door Ava stood beside and before walking out, he leaned near her ear and whispered the words, "They're always watching."

Abraham then opened the door and walked back into his shop, sitting down at the cash register.

But Ava had one last question.

She walked to the other side of the counter. They were still the only two in the store. Rain was now pouring outside so she didn't mind asking him out loud right where she stood.

"I have this. It was given to me by my late father," Ava grabbed her necklace that was tucked under her shirt and held the stone in her hand, presenting it in front of Abraham. The purple stone glowed before his eyes, both of which came into complete focus.

"I-is that…" he breathed, staring with a scared expression at the gem attached to Ava's necklace.

"My name is Ava Sinclair, and I believe that my ancestor was Anne Sinclair. If this is her dooming stone, and if your story is true, then I am the rightful heir to it," she spoke with a powerful tone. She wasn't quite sure how she suddenly obtained the courage to express herself as such for deep down she felt terrified.

Abraham's eyes shifted from the stone to Ava's eyes.

"You need to leave. Right now. You need to hide that stone and get out of this town immediately."

His tone had changed. He now sounded as scared as Ava was.

"Who else knows this story about Parkfield?" Ava yelled, not caring if people heard her from outside.

"Quiet down," he said in a hushed voice.

"No! I need to know! I keep getting stares and I think it's because of this necklace I've been wearing since I got here!" Ava squeezed her palm around the stone. "It's like everyone in this town knows about the story you just told and believes it!"

"Yes! Yes, everyone does know, and they most certainly believe it! If the wrong people get hold of you and what you possess, they could unleash the evil that has been locked away for centuries," he whispered, trying to calm her, "This town is full of descendants from Parkfield's earliest days and many of them have waited very patiently to see Esmerelda's plan fulfilled."

"Wouldn't it take the other three stones to unlock the barrier?"

"Ava, I believe there's a chance that they already have the other stones. They just need yours."

"They? Again, who are *they*?" Ava gasped, "And why the hell would people want to open the cave and unleash…Finis? Can't that evil creature kill us all? Please tell me, who are these people?"

"I can't tell you specifically who, just know that they are people around here that you'd least expect. People you have likely seen before. They are part of this. And earthly death is not a concern of theirs, they believe better things await them in the afterlife if they bring about the return of Finis. It's a death cult."

"Wait, then how does this all connect to Henry?" Ava asked.

Abraham paused as he checked the door for any potential incoming customers before saying in a low voice, "You should know by now that Henry's death was no accident, right?"

"Well, that's what everyone thinks, and there is evidence of foul play, but we still don't have a suspect," Ava said.

"Henry tried to take matters into his own hands and destroy the cave with explosives. I don't know if that would have even worked…but he was fighting against those who wish for this town's possible destiny to be fulfilled. He was followed up the mountain, strangled and then thrown off the cliff," Abraham said nonchalantly.

Ava was taken aback by how abruptly Abraham stated the death of Henry Van Scott as a certain fact.

"Who did it?" Ava asked.

"It could have been any of them, probably more than one. Lots of people in Parkfield are a part of this cult."

"H-how do you know?"

"Everyone in this town knows, but no one wants to tell the police the truth. In fact, some of the police might even be involved."

"But you're telling me. Why?"

Abraham turned to look out the windows and watch the rainfall that showed no sign of letting up.

"I had to tell someone who I thought might believe me. I had a feeling about you even before I saw the stone. No telling what my future holds. My time has been up for a while now."

"What do you mean?" Ava inquired.

Suddenly, a car pulled up on the curb in front of Abraham's shop and honked twice.

"Oh, that's my uncle," Ava sighed.

As Abraham continued to stare out the windows, a blank expression sprawled on his face. Wind from outside sounded like human screams, which made Ava more frightened.

"Alright then," Ava broke the awkward silence, "thank you for entrusting me with all of that information, sir."

She turned to take her leave until she heard Abraham's voice.

"Don't trust them, any of them," he warned.

Ava turned to look at the old man and saw that he was staring at her with a very serious expression.

She nodded before pushing open the front door, hearing the bell ding before stepping out of the store.

She scurried to her uncle's car, attempting to not get drenched by the pouring rain.

The window to the passenger's seat was rolled down just a little and inside was a grinning Uncle Matthew.

"Hey, Ava, get in!" he yelled waving, "Hurry up!"

Ava entered the vehicle and the noise from the wind and the rain hitting the earth quieted down.

"It sure is pouring again, the weather around here is strange," Matthew commented.

Ava buckled her seatbelt next to him. "Yeah, there's a lot around here that's strange."

"You were supposed to be at the diner. Did you not eat?"

"No, I…I wasn't hungry."

"I see you didn't buy anything from that weird store," Uncle Matthew said, "I was certain that you would, especially if you were in there the whole time. Did you see our friend Abraham?"

"Yes, he was there, but he didn't say much," Ava said, unsure what she should actually say to Uncle Matthew and what she should just keep to herself for now.

The car began moving, slowly departing from *SeEkS*. Ava looked back at the building; the shop looked as if it had grown darker inside. Maybe Abraham was closing up early and turning off the lights.

Perhaps if the rain wasn't pouring so hard, perhaps if the storm didn't blow in, they could've heard Abraham's screams from inside before they drove away.

Chapter Seven

It hadn't stopped raining since Ava had left Abraham's store, so she and her uncle stayed inside the hotel for the remainder of the day.

After making sure the curtains were completely closed and the door securely locked, Ava lay sprawled on her bed lazily flipping through TV channels. She didn't care what was on, she was just attempting to find something to get her mind off the fact that the gemstone around her neck might be the final key to unleashing damnation upon all of humanity. Not to mention that the entire town she was in may be in on it. She wanted to tell her uncle all of this but didn't really know how. What if none of what Abraham told her was true? She didn't want to take her uncle off his case over some crazy legend from an insane old man.

A knock on her door made her jump, immediately jolting her sense of fear into gear.

She approached the door and held her breath before looking through the peephole.

"Ava? You awake?"

Ava saw Uncle Matthew; her fear dispersed. She opened the door.

"Hey," Uncle Matthew started, his voice was deep and his normal happy nature seemed to have disappeared, "I need to talk to you."

Ava gulped. "S-sure,"

She stepped aside to allow her uncle to enter her room and shut and locked the door after he was inside.

He sat on the edge of her bed; one of his hands ran through his short hair. He seemed worried.

"What's the matter?" Ava asked.

"I just got a report that Abraham had been killed a few hours ago, basically right after we left his store," he sighed.

Ava couldn't breathe. She felt as if her heart stopped for a second.

"W-what?" Ava couldn't believe it. She had just talked to him. He was the one person she thought that she could trust in Parkfield—besides Uncle Matthew.

"Was there anyone else in the store with you while you were in there? Did you see anyone outside?"

"No, I was the only customer."

"You could have been in danger. Your life could have been in jeopardy and it would have been my fault for bringing you here…so, um," Uncle Matthew said as he frustratedly rubbed his temples trying to figure out what to do, "I need to go down to the department and see if we know anything else. You need to stay in your room. Lock your door and do not leave for any reason, alright?"

Ava nodded her head, unable to say anything.

"I am so sorry I brought you into this," Uncle Matthew said as he buried his hands in his face, "I didn't think this case would turn into what it has."

"It's okay, I'll be fine," Ava said attempting to comfort him.

Uncle Matthew shook his head, his hands still holding onto his face. "I need to take you home."

Ava couldn't protest. Abraham did tell her that the further she was from Parkfield, the safer she'd be.

"I need you to pack your things, I'm taking you home tomorrow."

"Okay," Ava agreed.

"I'll be back soon. Do *not* leave your room."

He stood up and approached the door but turned back to smile at Ava reassuringly.

"It'll all be okay, Ava."

She nodded with a smile.

He walked out of the room and shut the door behind him. She then locked the door and took in a shaky breath.

Who killed Abraham? And if they killed him soon after the conversation Abraham and I had, they must've heard what we were talking about. They must be a part of the crazy plan to release Finis, but who?

After about twenty minutes, another knock suddenly took Ava out of her thoughts and into a sinking feeling of paranoia.

She peeked through the peep hole. No one was there. All that stood in the dimly lit hallway were the strange paintings of clowns and farms and the doors leading to other rooms.

Ava lingered at the door for a while before she turned to go back to her bed. Then she stepped on something that wasn't carpet.

She removed her foot from the differently textured object and saw that it was a small slip of paper. She reached down to pick it up and noticed words written on it in very neat handwriting.

'I know how to destroy the gemstone. Meet me outside in the parking lot.'

Fear once again overtook her as she remembered the last words Abraham told her:

"Don't trust them, any of them,"

She reread the words numerous times, trying to think of what to do.

Perhaps I could simply look through the windows in the lobby, and if I see that the person in the parking lot doesn't look trustworthy, I can go back to my room and just stay put, she told herself.

The idea sufficed, so she placed the note on her dresser, grabbed her room key and exited her room.

Fear continued to run through her veins as she stepped carefully down the hallway, looking over her shoulder periodically. The lobby made her feel safer; a few other guests were having a pleasant-sounding conversation which calmed her nerves. There was no one behind the desk.

Large windows projected a pretty pink and orange sky as the sun began to set and rain clouds began to move out of the area. Ava studied the parking lot in front of the building.

With one fleeting glance, she spotted someone on a black motorcycle next to a car wearing a black hoodie, dark jeans and a black helmet that covered their face entirely.

As if by instinct, she walked through the exit doors and onto the concrete sidewalk leading to the parking lot.

The helmeted head of the mysterious figure on the motorcycle turned to see Ava approaching.

"Didn't think you'd show," he said in a low voice.

"Who are you? What do you know?" Ava asked, trying to act confident.

The man sighed before placing his hands on the helmet and swiftly pulled it off.

Out of every image that ran through her mind as to who he might've looked like, no picture closely resembled how he actually looked. His dark hair was slicked back, his pale, gray eyes watched hers in a curious manner, looking as if he was trying to figure her out.

She also noticed the two red stripes on the side of the motorcycle, it was the exact one she saw in the parking lot that same day. She knew who this man was.

"You're Chief Sean." Ava stated. A breeze suddenly flew past her as she folded her arms over her chest from the chill.

He simply nodded and continued to stare at her. She felt as if he was looking into her soul.

The chief moved his pointer and middle finger indicating for her to come closer.

Ava's breath hitched, and a feeling of uncertainty washed over her. She doesn't know this man at all, and especially if he knows that she has the last stone, he could possibly be with the cult. She had to remain cautious and careful.

"I'm here to help you, I promise," he said staring at the empty road in front of them.

Ava took a deep breath. Surprisingly, she lowered her guard almost immediately and slowly walked closer to him. Her footsteps filled the silent void of the parking lot left by the hiss of a passing car. She stepped in small puddles that had been left by the recent rain as water splashed onto her feet. Not that she minded, she wasn't in the headspace to worry about anything else other than her current situation with this man and what he knew that could possibly help.

In a matter of seconds, she stood a few feet from him, breathing in his cologne that lingered in the air…calming scents of cedar and musk which made Ava relax a little bit.

"Get on," Sean said.

"W-what?" Ava was taken aback.

"You heard me," he said nonchalantly as he surveyed the area around them.

"Look, I'm not supposed to leave here. Uncle Matthew told me to stay put. I-I don't even know you," Ava stated.

"Listen to me," he said sternly as he took his haunting, gray eyes off of the surroundings in front of them and glared at her, "I know you know the legend of this town and yes, it's all true. I'm the only person who will tell you how to destroy that damned stone and end this curse for good. We have to go where no one can find us and we can't be followed. So, you can either climb on now, go with me and let me explain how you can get out of this mess, or you can continue being ignorant and get yourself and your loved ones killed. So, which will it be, sweetheart?"

Ava knew that she had no choice. She needed this man's help. She needed to know where she fit in all of this. Even though leaving went against what her uncle told her, she felt that she was in way too deep and had to see where this would lead her.

Without answering, she carefully climbed onto the motorcycle.

Sean didn't turn around to face her, he simply moved his arm back to hand her the dark helmet he was wearing earlier.

She cautiously grasped the heavy headpiece and slowly put it over her head. A small, glass shield covered her face when the helmet was completely on her head and she adjusted it so she could fully see.

Ava had never sat on a motorcycle, much less ridden on one, either. Her life had never been filled with much adventure; the most spontaneous thing she'd done was choose a cream cheese muffin over the low fat one back when she was thirteen. So, doing something remotely out of those boundaries was like exploring undiscovered territory.

A sharp revving of the motor scared and excited Ava. Out of fright, she flung her arms around the chief's waist, clutching on for dear life.

"Hang on," he said as the wheels beneath them spun forward sending Ava into a voyage of exhilaration.

Ava squealed out of shock at the fast pace they were traveling. Streetlamps flew past them providing visibility to the road under the dying sky. The motorcycle moved at impossibly fast speeds. Within minutes, the two had flown past the town square.

The night sky was clearing, and the visible, pinkish moon was almost full, shining down on Ava and the chief. Stars presented themselves as the clouds passed, sparkling brightly as if attempting to overpower the light projected by the moon.

Through strands of her hair and the face shield of the helmet, Ava stared at the mysterious man that she was clinging to. His smell lingered in the helmet and was intoxicatingly sweet, reminding her of how she had dreamt her dream boy might smell. And with her arms clutched tightly around him, she could feel that he was quite muscular.

He's like, almost thirty. Don't think about stuff like that. Ava shamed herself in her mind.

It never really dawned on her as to where they were going until they drove past all of Parkfield, now making their way onto the mountain highway.

"Where are we going?" Ava yelled over the wind.

"Somewhere safe," he yelled back.

"Don't trust them, any of them," she remembered Abraham saying to her. Poor Abraham…

Ava felt uncertain for the rest of the drive, glancing back at the distant buildings of Parkfield that now looked like pieces of a miniature town. She fixed her eyes on what looked to be the police department, wondering about Uncle Matthew and how mad he would be if he found out that she left against his wishes.

They finally reached the end of the mountain, trees layered on top of trees until they formed a dark forest. The chief pulled to the side of the road and climbed off of his motorcycle.

"Is this the place?" Ava asked pulling the helmet off of her head. She realized that helmets tend to mess up hair and suddenly wished that a hairbrush was nearby.

Sean nodded and held out his hand, beckoning her to take it in order to climb off of the bike safely. Ava stared at the offer; feeling as if she were in a romance movie of some sort, and eventually placed the helmet on her seat and grasped his hand as she stepped off the motorcycle.

When she dismounted onto the grass, she noticed she hadn't let go of his hand. She was sure he noticed this too, but he didn't remove his hand from hers either.

The sound of crickets began to chirp, demanding to be heard. Ava stared at the mysterious man, noticing his beautiful pale eyes that lit up from the moonlight. She looked up at him, once again greeting his eyes; but this time, he was looking at her, too.

She was unsure of what feelings she had formed, a mix of euphoria and longing…excitement and caution.

The act of simply staring at each other progressed for another few seconds, until Sean purposely cleared his throat. Ava immediately whipped her hand away, feeling embarrassed.

"Sorry," she muttered, holding her hands together awkwardly.

"I'll show you the place," he said disregarding her apology He turned on a flashlight and walked towards an opening in the many trees that stood before them.

Ava stood with uncertainty, unsure if she should follow him into the dark and mysterious wooded area. But she knew that standing next to an empty highway at night wouldn't be any safer than following the attractive man into the forest. He was a police chief after all…

So, she followed him.

The forest was exactly how she'd expected it would be; a dark, mysterious and almost enchanting place. Sean walked in front of her, climbing over logs occasionally and moving any fallen branches that had fallen upon the path. Ava turned around, noticing that she could no longer see the edge of the highway or his motorcycle. She could only see the dark forest that swallowed her up more and more with each step.

She noticed that she was breaking into a sweat, the amount of walking had her legs feeling weak and tired.

"Are we almost there?" she breathed from behind him.

"Yes," he said.

That's when Ava noticed the trees opening up creating a small space of land. In the light of Sean's flashlight, she saw an old, uninviting cabin with a small wooden door in the front. A brick chimney jutted out from a rusted, tin roof. A pathway led the two to the front door. With each step Ava felt her fears strangely dissolve. They were truly in the middle of nowhere, she didn't think that anyone could or would be able to find them here. If Sean is to be trusted, he could safely tell her how to destroy the crystal and bring an end to this nightmare.

"How do you know about this place?" Ava inquired.

He didn't respond. Instead, he slowly opened the wooden door causing old and worn hinges to complain with an awful squeak. Ava thanked him before stepping inside. The dark cabin had only one room; a small red sofa faced a brick fireplace and a wooden table with chairs sat in front of a square window. The moonlight revealed some bookshelves in a corner of the room; each shelf crammed with dusty books with likely beautiful words on each page. The room was dark. Electricity here was highly doubtful. Used candles sat on the table along with a book of matches.

She heard Sean enter the room and the heavy wooden door shut.

Ava turned around, meeting him. "So, now what?"

Sean struck a match and began to light a few candles. The flames from the candles moved in a sort of dance, almost synchronizing with Sean's soft voice as he spoke.

"I've never believed in the supernatural," he said as he pulled out one of the chairs and sat down, beckoning Ava to sit by moving his pointer and middle fingers.

Ava felt her cheeks tinting into a light pink, but the room was hopefully too dark for him to notice. She sat in the other chair, staring at the man.

"Stories about ghosts and witches and things like that have never sparked an interest in me," he said watching the lit candles that sat between them, "That was until the death of Henry Van Scott." He paused to light one more candle on the table. "I'm not originally from here, I'm from Pittsburg, but there's a reason why I moved from the big city to such a small, unknown town. It's because of a story my great-grandfather told me when I was younger. He told me how when he was a young boy he lived in this very town. He told me the whole story about Finis and Esmerelda, the coven and so forth. And then presented me a gemstone, and claimed that it belonged to one of the four witches, and that I am her descendant."

"S-so you're saying that you have..." Ava started, horrified by what he was telling her.

Sean reached into his pocket and pulled out a small drawstring bag. He opened it and revealed a small stone. It shined an orange-yellow glow with white specks and was shaped exactly like Ava's.

Her mouth hung agape.

"A-And you're sure th-that this is real?" Ava stuttered.

"Well, yes. It doesn't identify with any known gems or stones," Sean said, "It fits the description of Anne Yorke's dooming stone, and as it turns out, I am a direct descendent of Anne Yorke. Let me see your gemstone, I know it's around your neck."

Ava stopped for a split second and almost felt like she should make a run for it…but instead she complied and raised her necklace from out of her shirt. The purple glow seemed stronger than usual and was at the same intensity of Sean's stone.

"Amazing…the fourth dooming stone," Sean said in almost a whisper.

"This is crazy," Ava said, pushing her hair out of her face, "Y-you need to leave. You're in danger! There are people looking for you, a-and with two of the four stones here, if they have possession of the other two, those crazy people will be able to free Finis."

"You're worried about me?"

He leaned back in his chair, crossing his arms together with a smirk.

"Well, yeah. I just don't want to see anyone else getting hurt from this."

Ava swallowed, hoping that Sean didn't see right through her. Of course, she didn't want to see anyone else get hurt from this, but what meant was that she didn't anything to happen to Sean.

"Hmm," he said with the smirk never leaving his face, "So, you care about my safety?"

"Sure, I care about everyone's safety," Ava chuckled, nervously trying to find a way out of this awkward situation.

He didn't say anything, he simply continued to watch her with a sly smile.

Silence began to form around them, and Ava almost forgot what she had come here for.

"So, aren't you going to tell me how to destroy it?" she asked, rubbing her neck awkwardly.

"Oh, of course," he said, the smile dropping from his lips. He ran his fingers through his silky black hair as he got up with his flashlight and moved towards one of the bookshelves against the wall.

"There is a book here that describes how you have to go about it…I need you to read it."

"Why haven't you tried destroying yours yet?"

"That wouldn't do the trick. Each of our ancestors made the dooming stones at different times; yours made her stone first, and mine made hers afterwards. It turns out they can only be destroyed in the order in which they were created. But once the first one is gone, the others have no power anymore. It is written that yours is the first made, so you have to be the one to do this."

"Oh," Ava mumbled, still trying to wrap her head around everything.

Sean began scanning the many books until he spotted one with a crimson spine and gently pulled it out of the shelf.

As he walked back to the table, he placed the book in front of Ava.

"Well, how do I destroy my stone?" Ava asked, sounding a bit ruder than she intended.

He opened the crimson book to the first page, avoiding the flames cast by the candles.

"What is this?" Ava asked, looking up at Sean.

"Read it and you'll understand," he said.

Ava looked back down at the book and began reading the handwritten words:

Isabelle Sinclair, daughter of Anne Sinclair, 1711.

She gasped and glanced up at Sean, confusion whirled around her. He nodded, answering the unspoken question.

This must have been her great, great, grandmother's diary, Ava was an heir to the stone after all.

"This is crazy," Ava repeated as she continued flipping through the pages, passing many dates starting in January and going through June. That's when the passages abruptly ended, leaving the rest of the diary empty.

"W-what happened to the rest of the entries?" Ava asked. In the final entry, Ava noticed a difference in the handwriting. In the first entry, her handwriting seemed neat and careful, while the final entry seemed sloppy and rushed.

"The last entry is all you need to read to understand what is at stake," Sean said solemnly.

Ava began to read.

June 12th, 1711

I am to destroy the first cast dooming stone, the Sinclair stone. I possess the power to do it but I am frightened. I do not wish to die.

Ava looked at Sean, worry now flooding her eyes.

"Go on, keep reading," he said.

She continued reading the passage.

If future descendants find this, if you are reading these entries, if I have failed to destroy the stone and you or someone in our family line has acquired it, understand, it must be destroyed.

Note the following words carefully: the only way to abolish the dooming stone and thereby render all dooming stones useless is to die with it in your possession. There is no other way. If the other stones are gathered at Mount Redlock and this stone is still in existence, the possibility of unleashing Esmerelda and Finis remains. Please, you must gather the courage that I couldn't. This is my final entry and decree. I am sincerely remorseful that I could not bring myself to do what was needed and am ashamed of my cowardice. Please forgive me and may God have mercy on my soul,

Isabelle Sinclair

Chapter Eight

"No!" Ava shot up from the seat, throwing the diary on the table. "I'm not going to kill myself to destroy this stone! I couldn't do that to my uncle!"

"Look, I know that it's a lot to take in, but it's the only way," Sean said rising from his seat and slowly walking over to Ava, "That…that thing has the potential to kill us all," he said as he pointed in the direction of the mountain where Finis patiently waited, "You have to, or else we will all die."

Ava felt herself tear up, knowing that she was destined for this and that she had to do it. The stakes were too high.

"Our lives are in your hands, and I'm so sorry that they are," Sean said as he took both of Ava's shaky hands into his, "You don't deserve this."

A tear slipped from Ava's eye.

"I don't want to die," she whispered.

"I know," he said taking one of his hands and wiping the tear from her cheek, "It's gonna be okay."

"You promise?" Ava cried.

"I promise," he whispered, before wrapping his arms around her waist, holding her close.

Ava instinctively put her arms around his neck, crying into his shoulder.

"Look," he said as he released his grip from her, "the blood moon will appear in two days, so you don't have much time left."

Ava took a shaky breath in.

"I-I need to say goodbye to my uncle. I need to see him one last time," she cried.

"Of course," Sean said in a soft, comforting voice, "you should do that now. I need to get back to the station anyway."

Ava wiped her tears from her face and nodded.

"Could I take the diary with me?" she asked.

"Actually," Sean took the book from the table. "I need to hold onto it, there are passages in there that concern my ancestors too."

"Oh," Ava sniffed, her eyes fixated on the floor.

"Well, we should get going," he said as he placed the diary back into the bookshelf.

Ava headed towards the door, unaware of the chattering voices coming from outside.

"Let me get the door for you," Sean walked towards the door.

Then Ava heard the voices as they almost erupted from outside and a warm, flickering glow was shining thought the cracks in the door. Ava looked at Sean with confusion.

"Sean, what's going on?" Ava asked, worriedly.

"Ava," Sean said as his face cringed with guilt and remorse, "I'm sorry."

Sean then opened the door and around forty people stood in the front yard of the cabin each carrying a lit torch. Two were holding a large wooden rectangular sized box about the size of a coffin. All Ava could hear were chants and yelling. She turned to Sean, who couldn't bring himself to look at Ava.

"Sean, what the hell is happening? Who are all these people?" Ava's voice cracked, for she knew that she had been betrayed.

"Forgive me," he muttered before walking towards the crowd of people.

"Sean! Wait!" Ava pleaded. People began walking towards her as fire from the torches engulfed her eyes.

She stood at the doorway cowering, unable to breathe. She tried to move, but her muscles stayed stiff. Tears escaped her eyes as she watched the crowd begin to close in on her.

Ava had only felt this way in one other moment of her life: the second before the car crash. She hated the feeling of impending doom that was out of her control. She had to do something but she wasn't able to move a muscle.

Finally, she forced her way through her paralysis and quickly shut the front door and locked it.

"Surround the cabin! Break the windows!" she heard someone yell from outside.

Ava's heart was racing, her eyes welled up with more tears as she crouched next to the bookshelf in the corner. Light from the torches held by the crowd bled into the room. When the light was so bright that the room seemed completely lit up, she knew her time was about to run out.

Though she couldn't comprehend what she was doing, she located her ancestor's diary from the bookshelf and ran over to the table.

I need to write Uncle Matthew a note, Ava thought to herself.

"In five, men!" she suddenly heard someone yell at the front door.

"Five!" he yelled.

Ava grabbed Abraham's pen from her back pocket and scribbled down a brief, six-word message to her uncle as quickly as she could.

"Four!"

She closed the diary shut and placed it back onto the bookshelf upside down making sure to not push the book completely back in, trying to make it stand out in case her uncle ever found this cabin.

"Three!"

Ava took multiple shaky breaths in, awaiting her fate. The smell of lavender tea filled her nose again. There was no time to try to figure out why or even give it a second thought.

"Two!"

She shut her eyes, horrified by what the people may do.

"One!"

The cabin door suddenly broke open and a strong hand grasped hers, pulling her out the cabin and through the large mob.

She flung her eyes open, noticing that she was now running with this person in the forest. The insects were screaming as if for help and were nearly as loud as the voices ringing from behind her.

It was completely dark and difficult to see through the forest, especially with someone tugging her in random directions through the woods, forcing her to adapt to the sudden turns and twists.

She couldn't tell who grabbed her, afraid that perhaps this person was going to kill her; but she knew that she'd rather die without a crowd of crazy people cheering on her death. And though it was dark, except for the sweeping beam of his flashlight, she noticed his familiar dark black hair.

They finally made it out of the woods, with leaves and tiny pieces of sticks clasping onto their clothes and hair. Ava fell onto the grass before the road, gasping for breath. They were now at the edge of the highway where the motorcycle was parked. But she also noticed several more vehicles including a black van with dark, tinted windows parked in front of Sean's motorcycle. She looked up to see Sean standing above her.

"Are you alright?" Sean turned to look down at Ava.

"You—you traitor!" Ava gasped, "What do you want from me?"

"Ava, please, let me explain," Sean said softly.

"No!" Ava shot up from the ground. "You tricked me! I thought I could trust you!"

"Please, just listen, they are coming!" Sean began, attempting to touch her arm with comfort.

"No! Don't touch me, you jerk!" Ava stepped away from him, "What you told me at that cabin, the diary, was any of that even true?"

"Yes, it's all true."

"Then why did you sell me out?"

Thunder crashed from arriving dark clouds of yet another storm. Rain immediately began to fall. Within seconds, the two were drenched.

"They forced me to!" Sean threw his arms out in frustration. "They were going to kill me if I didn't! But I did want you to know about how to destroy the stone, and you now know."

"So, you'd rather let me die at the hands of the mob?" Ava ran her fingers through her hair angrily.

"No, I wouldn't, and that's why I'm doing this," Sean said, lowering his tone.

"Doing what?"

Ava still spoke in an angered tone but was secretly curious as to what he was implying.

Without responding, Sean turned towards the road and quickly led her by her arm to his motorcycle.

"What are you doing, Sean?"

"Get on and grab the handlebars," he said, "Hurry!"

"Are you insane? I don't know how to drive one of these things!"

"They'll be here any minute, their torches must be out from the rain but they're coming."

Sean then looked directly at her and said, "Do you trust me?"

And unfortunately, she knew that she still did. She really didn't know of any other option.

Ava scoffed as she stepped to the bike. Sean helped her onto the seat.

"Thank you," he said as he placed his helmet on her head and kicked up the kickstand.

Small beads of water attached themselves to his thick eyelashes like a cobweb. And whenever he'd look at her, she felt as if he was reading into her past, understanding her like no one else possibly could.

His soft pink lips curled into a sad smile; his eyes crinkled with sadness.

"What?" Ava asked, confused by his expression.

"I am sorry, Ava," Sean said quietly, but loud enough for her to hear.

"I know," she smiled reassuringly at him. She didn't exactly forgive him, but she knew that he meant what he said.

"It's been an honor to know you, even if it was only for a little while," he said.

"Sean, what now?" Ava asked worriedly, "what exactly am I supposed to do?"

"I want you to take this motorcycle and drive as carefully and as quickly as you can. I don't need to start it, but I will put the headlight on. Just coast down the mountain like you're on a big bicycle. Put the hand brake on when you need to and just roll down into Parkfield. It's the easiest way."

"Sean, stop messing around," Ava chuckled nervously. "We both need to get away from those insane people. And I would most definitely crash your motorcycle driving it on my own."

"I'm so glad I met you, Ava," his voice cracked slightly.

"Sean what are you doing? Get on, this isn't funny. We need to leave now."

Ava raised her voice slightly, afraid now that the cult members were close by and would hear her if she yelled.

"Goodbye, Ava Sinclair," he smiled at her and slowly walked away.

"Sean, get back here!" Ava yelled, "Sean!"

He headed towards the forest as a few flashlights appeared from the edge of the woods, getting brighter and brighter.

Sean stood next to the opening; Ava finally noticed the figures holding flashlights trudging closer to him.

"Please, Sean, come back!" Ava begged to herself.

A crowd of people soon gathered from the woods to where Sean stood.

Sean turned around and looked at her with a reassuring smile and nodded.

And suddenly, though the rain was loud, a sharp noise overpowered the incessant pouring of water.

She shrieked as she watched Sean's body collapse on the ground clutching his chest.

"There she is!" she heard someone yell.

Her instincts kicked in as she gripped the handlebar and shoved off down the treacherous mountain road.

Ava screamed, confused by everything that had taken place. She was unsure on how to steer without slipping but kept the bike under control. The headlight revealed only a few feet of rain drenched road in front of her. After what seemed like miles, she was able to navigate turns and began getting the hang of controlling the motorcycle.

And though she thought that she was far enough away, she knew that the other vehicles up there would not stay parked for long. As soon as that thought crossed her mind, she noticed the white glow of headlights growing in her circular rearview mirror.

Ava turned her head and saw the large black van tailgating her. It picked up speed and switched to the lane next to her, gradually getting closer and closer. People were hanging out of the window, taunting her.

Ava let off the brake and picked up the pace, hoping that she could outrun them and make it to Parkfield. The vehicles now drove side-by-side; Ava wasn't sure if speeding up would be the right idea, for no matter how fast she went she knew that they would inevitably catch up to her. That, and she would likely lose control and crash.

Suddenly, the man in the passenger seat yelled out of his window, "Why keep trying to run from us? She will get what she wants no matter what!"

Ava ignored him, fixating her eyes on the road in front of her.

Finally, both vehicles passed the sign that read *Welcome to Parkfield.*

She knew that by taking one more turn, she would roll down the hill into Parkfield. She was so close to safety. To Uncle Matthew.

But the turn was a very sharp one, and with the rain and the speed she was going, the motorcycle slipped on the wet road and sent her into a skid.

Hard asphalt skinned her arms and legs as she rolled into the grass; she felt pain everywhere.

The black van came to a screeching halt.

Ava laid on the ground, unable to feel or breathe. And though Sean's helmet provided protection for her head, she believed that she might have a slight concussion.

All doors to the van opened; the two at the back of the van, two sliding doors, and the two front passenger doors. At least eight people somehow piled out of the van, each wearing grey or black clothing.

They began to surround Ava who still lay on the ground, each with an expression of pure evil.

"Grab her," she heard one of them say.

Immediately, one of the mysterious figures picked her up bridal-style and carried her over to the van. Everyone followed.

Ava knew she couldn't do anything now to prevent her fate. She let everyone down. Especially Uncle Matthew.

Oh no, Uncle Matthew, she thought to herself.

The man carrying her placed her inside the dark vehicle. Everyone piled inside and the van drove off down the road.

"Please, let me go," Ava whispered. It hurt to even speak.

None of them responded to her, instead, one of them grabbed a backpack and pulled out what looked to be a hypodermic needle. They tightly grabbed Ava's left arm before injecting the liquid into her. Ava winced in pain.

Her mind became foggy, and in seconds, she lost complete consciousness.

Chapter Nine

"Ava, Ava Sinclair," Matthew said again knocking on her motel room door, "Are you in there?"

There was no response.

"Where is that girl?" he whispered to himself with annoyance and concern.

He looked around the dark hallway; it was completely deserted and quiet aside from the soft music that played from the lobby.

Uncle Matthew took a deep breath before walking into the cozy, yet empty, lobby. He turned to the front desk where a young man sat reading a book. It wasn't the same man from yesterday; this man had dark red curly hair, light blue eyes and wore a white collared shirt with a brown vest. And because he looked like he was only in his twenties, Uncle Matthew was surprised by his vintage-like style.

"Excuse me," Uncle Matthew said approaching the desk where the man looked up at him with speculation.

"Yes?" the man replied.

"My daughter is staying in room fourteen, but she isn't answering the door when I knocked."

"Oh, Okay."

The red head grabbed a list of papers and flipped through them.

"Ava Sinclair?" he read aloud.

"Yes," Uncle Matthew sighed, "she promised me that she would be staying in her hotel room for the whole night, and it isn't like her to disobey me."

"Uh huh," the front desk man said with little interest, looking as if he were back to reading his book.

"Sir, please, would you mind unlocking her door? I'm her father, I'm staying in room thirteen. Look, I'm worried. I'm sure you've heard of the recent deaths in town."

"Are you…Matthew Sinclair?" the man said looking at the ledger.

"Yes."

"Alright, here."

He handed Uncle Matthew a key.

"Bring it back when you're done," he said

"Thank you so much," Uncle Matthew said. The man simply shrugged and continued reading.

Matthew quickly ran to room fourteen, inserted the key and opened the door.

The room was messy; Ava's clothes were scattered all over her unmade bed.

"Ava?" he said as he walked around attempting to find any sign of her, "Are you here?"

He checked the empty bathroom. Sweat began to appear on his face.

"Where is she?" he mumbled worriedly.

That's when he noticed the small slip of paper that sat folded on top of Ava's dresser.

Out of curiosity, Uncle Matthew walked over to her dresser and picked it up to read.

Within seconds, Uncle Matthew placed the paper in his pocket and raced out of the room, terror in his eyes.

He ran to the front desk, startling the red-haired man enough to make him put his book down and look curiously at Uncle Matthew.

"Is there a problem?" he asked with a monotone voice.

"Ava wasn't in there!" Uncle Matthew slammed the spare key to her room on the front desk.

"Okay, maybe she's somewhere in town," the clerk sighed, clearly annoyed that he's actually having to deal with an issue while on the job.

"She-she left with some man in the parking lot!" Matthew fumed.

"Calm down, sir, I'm sure she's fine," the man said only in an attempt to get Uncle Matthew to leave him alone.

"Please, did you see anyone suspicious in the parking lot? A vehicle not belonging to a motel guest? Anything?"

The man at the desk thought for a moment, before sighing and setting his book down.

"Do you have a picture of her?" he asked.

"Yes, yes I do," Uncle Matthew reached to his back pocket and pulled out his brown leather wallet. He flipped through his credit cards and cash until he pulled out a folded image. "Here, that's her."

Uncle Matthew handed the man the photo, and the man unfolded it to find two smiling faces in front of what looked to be a university with brown brick and pretty landscaping. One of the faces belonged to Uncle Matthew, while the other belonged to Ava.

"That was taken almost a year ago," Uncle Matthew said as a smile formed on his lips, "I was helping her move into her college dorm. She'd just gotten into Harvard. I was so proud of her."

"Mhm," the man mumbled as he inspected the picture, "Yeah, I saw her about three hours ago."

He handed the picture back to Uncle Matthew.

"You did?" Uncle Matthew asked as he placed the photo back into his wallet carefully and slipped the wallet into his back pocket, "Well, what did you see?"

"Some guy with a black motorcycle picked her up and drove towards the town, I don't know what he looked like."

"Did you notice anything about the motorcycle?" description.

"Uh, it had a big, red stripe. I think," he shrugged.

"A big, red stripe?"

Uncle Matthew immediately knew who took Ava. Chief Sean.

Proper parking wasn't the first thing on Uncle Matthew's mind as he sped through the rain into the police department parking lot. After screeching to a stop, he ended up taking two spaces in front of the building. Of course, being this late at night, not many cars were present. One vehicle he noticed missing was Sean's motorcycle.

As Matthew scrambled into the building he was greeted by Jacob.

"Matthew? Why, you can't stay away from the department for a seco—"

"Do you know where Sean is?" Matthew demanded.

"Uh, the chief? Probably at his house I would guess."

Jacob was a bit concerned about Uncle Matthew's tone.

"He said he wasn't going home," a woman in a police uniform said from the front desk, a cup of coffee in her hand.

"Did he say where he would be?" Uncle Matthew asked the woman.

"I don't know," she shrugged, sipping her coffee.

"What's the problem, Matthew? Why are you so worked up?" Jacob asked.

"It's…nothing. Just, let me know if he comes back here. You're on night duty tonight, right?" Uncle Matthew inquired, placing his hand on his forehead as if a headache was setting in.

"I sure am, here 'til dawn," Jacob said, "I'll ring your motel in the morning when he gets in."

"Thank you," Uncle Matthew said as the sides of his lips twisted into a false smile. He knew he couldn't wait until morning.

"Of course, that's what buddies are for—" Jacob abruptly stopped speaking after Uncle Matthew suddenly ran out of the building. Jacob watched through the large windows as he hastily got into his car and drove off.

The first thing Ava noticed when she came to were the ropes that kept her from escaping the heavy oak chair she was sitting on. The room was dark, and she appeared to be alone. Even though light was limited; she knew that the room was big. Mainly because whenever she attempted to scream through the cloth wrapped around her mouth, her muffled voice echoed. Her head still hurt but overall, she felt better than she did when she wrecked.

One light hung above her, which flickered occasionally. Bugs flew around the light and made small noises whenever they accidently bumped into the lightbulb itself.

Although Ava knew that it was doubtful that anyone could hear her, she continued to yell with the cloth wrapped around her mouth. She struggled to untie herself, but it was no use.

"Will you shut up?" someone yelled.

Ava turned to the direction of the voice and watched as a man entered the room through a distant doorway which led to the outside. Through the dark she could see a thick cluster of trees through the doorway. She was being held captive somewhere in the middle of a forest. But before she could get a better view of the surrounding area, the man shut the door.

"We've been waiting for you for quite a while, Ava Sinclair," the man dressed in all black said.

Ava tried speaking but any words were unidentifiable.

"Don't try talking, please," he said closing in on her. He pulled out a small medical bag and retrieved a needle. After inspecting the shot, he suddenly injected it into her arm.

Ava screamed, but all that came out was a loud muffle.

"Oh, get over it," he said placing the emptied shot back into his small case, "It'll keep you calm during your stay here."

Due to the lack of light, Ava couldn't identify who this man was. His voice sounded familiar, but Ava still couldn't tell.

"I'm sure you have lots of questions," he began, "And I promise that soon they will all be answered."

Ava gave the man a strange look.

"Oh, and yes, I should probably remove the cloth around your mouth now," the man said as he walked behind Ava's chair.

She could feel his cold hands untie the knot that held the cloth in place. The second she knew it was completely untied, she spat out the white cloth and began to scream.

"Help! Help, please! Please, let me go! I've got to get out of here!" Ava yelled as loud as she could, making the man behind her cover her mouth with his hand.

"Will you stop yelling? God, you're an annoying one," he seethed.

Ava finally settled down, gasping for breath; his icy fingers curled around her mouth.

"You good now?" he asked.

She nodded.

The man removed his hand from her mouth and walked around her chair standing directly in front of her in the light.

It took Ava a moment to realize who this was, until she remembered the strange man at the front desk at the motel.

It was him.

"Where's Sean?" Ava inquired; worry filled her voice.

"You mean that traitor? He's dead."

He smiled sickly sweet which made Ava shiver with fear.

"Just take my stone, okay? Let me go; I won't tell." Ava begged. She knew that these people were capable of almost anything.

"Oh, we have your stone already," the man said.

Ava then realized that her necklace was gone.

"And after everything you now know and everything you've witnessed? Not a chance. Besides, we still need you…c'mon now, why would you still be alive unless we needed you for something?"

Though Ava was horrified at what he just said, it did make sense.

"Please don't hurt my uncle."

Ava felt tears form in her eyes. The ropes that gripped her wrists stung almost as much as her skinned-up arms and legs.

"Oh, Ava," he laughed shaking his head, "And we thought you were smart because you go to an Ivy League school. As it turns out, you're just plain stupid."

"Hey," Ava protested, her eyebrows furrowed with anger.

"We won't personally hurt your uncle, or anyone else for that matter, but they're all gonna die anyway, including you."

"You're crazy if you want to release Finis and kill everyone in the world!" Ava yelled.

"So, you *have* done your research. Good for you, young detective! You probably got your intel from Abraham…he was an easy one to get rid of," he said smiling.

A look of horror came over Ava's face upon his admission as he continued talking.

"This world is overpopulated. Way too many of us, and most don't even deserve to be here. The earth cannot sustain it. It's time to start over."

"Look," said Ava, "I know that there are a lot of people in this world both good and bad, but if this really happens, we're *all* going to die. Including you!"

"And I'm okay with that!" he said raising his voice and throwing his arms out, "I'd rather die and give the world back to its original spirits than have to live in this sorry excuse for a planet! Esmerelda gave us a chance to start over, and I, as well as all of her followers, can't thank her enough for that!"

"But this is insane!" she yelled fuming, "You're willing to die for nothing!"

"That's a lie! All of us, since the beginning of time, have been sinners. This world has been filled with cruelty and evil for as long as history has been written. We have all committed sin and continue to without any real consequence. Do you really think I haven't done something bad? Of course, I have, I have killed people! But it was all for a good cause, I believe God will reward me once Finis is released and I will live on in paradise instead of this wretched world. The time of man on this planet is coming to its inevitable end!"

"You're crazy," Ava said breathing heavily.

"You'll understand soon, Ava Sinclair. Now I must be going, there are more preparations to be made before the blood moon."

He opened the door he first entered from and exited the warehouse. "Oh," he peeked his head back inside for a moment, "and scream all you want. You're deep in the forest so only the bugs will hear you. And enjoy the drug I just gave you; it should mellow you out quite a bit."

She let out a shaky breath as the door shut, tears still streamed down her face. In seconds, she began feeling drowsy and shut her eyes, passing out in a restless slumber.

The gravel shook Uncle Matthew's car as he drove at a rapid pace down Sean's driveway. His house was modest,

white-washed brick walls and a worn, discolored shingled roof.
A typical Parkfield home.

Matthew parked his car, stepped out of his vehicle and
shut the door behind him. The rain had let up and the only light
that could be seen was a flood light in the front of the house.
Inside the house was as dark as the night sky.

Uncle Matthew approached Sean's doorstep.

"Sean?" he said as he knocked on the red front door; the
paint was slightly chipped and looked old, "Are you in there?
We need to talk." Uncle Matthew rang the doorbell several
times until he figured that no one could possibly have the
patience to not answer the door by now. He sighed before
departing from the house.

That was until he heard shuffling from behind him.

He whipped around, but no one was there.

"Hello?" Uncle Matthew said in almost a yell. He placed
his hand on his gun just in case he needed it.

He shrugged off the odd noise and proceeded back to his
car.

"Matthew?" someone said from behind him.

Uncle Matthew turned around to see Jacob wearing a
hoodie over his uniform exiting Sean's front door.

"Jacob? You scared me!" Uncle Matthew laughed,
"Why are you here…and how did you get here so fast?"

"You told me to look for Sean, remember? I tried calling
but there was no answer, and there's nothing going on at the
station right now, so I came over here…"

"You're lying," Uncle Matthew said to Jacob with a cold
expression, "Look, if Sean's not in there, you tell me where he
is. You know, don't you? I think he has Ava with him!"

Jacob stared directly at Matthew and spoke in a strict
tone that he had never heard him use before. "Matthew, I need
you to stay away, okay? You don't want to know where Sean
is. I don't want you to get hurt, so please, leave while you can."

"What are you talking about, Jacob?" Uncle Matthew's face was filled with confusion.

Jacob didn't respond. He simply put his hands in his hoodie pockets and avoided eye contact.

"Where is Sean, Jacob? I believe Ava ran off with him somewhere, I have a witness who says as much."

"Sean is dead!" Jacob yelled.

"What?" Uncle Matthew whispered, unable to comprehend the words that Jacob said.

"He's dead, Matthew," Jacob sighed, lowering his tone almost immediately, "And you'll end up just like him if you don't leave this town right now."

"Look, I don't know why you're suddenly acting so bizarre and making up stories of your chief being dead, but it isn't funny, Jacob. I need to find Ava. Now, tell me where he is. Where is he?! Where is Ava?!" Uncle Matthew shouted.

"Fine. There's not much time left anyway. If you don't believe me, go up to right around mile marker seventeen on the mountain highway, you'll find Chief Sean's body on the side of the road."

"Jacob, what the hell are you even talking about?" Uncle Matthew raised his voice even louder, "Where is Ava?"

"Ava is fine for now, but I can't tell you where she is," Jacob said, "I'm sorry."

"Why? What is happening?" Uncle Matthew said confused and frustrated.

"Go where I told you to go, find out for yourself. But I suggest you hurry. I'm going back to the station in a while, I just want to get some things," Jacob said as he entered Sean's house, gave Matthew one last look and closed the door.

Fear and worry flooded Uncle Matthew's entire being as he jumped back into his car and flew down the dark road. Bugs stopped chirping and all of nature's sounds ceased. The world outside seemed to fall completely silent like it knew something was coming.

Matthew's face felt numb, all he could focus on was the road that laid ahead of him, supposedly leading him to the chief's body. As he exited onto the mountain road, he saw Chief Sean's wrecked motorcycle. He stopped to inspect but there was no sign of anyone around. Continuing up the road, he grasped the steering wheel tightly, praying that perhaps this was all a sick joke that Jacob made up. But he knew that Jacob wouldn't go that far. Headlights allowed him to see only a little; and for the rest of the drive, everything was dead quiet.

When Matthew arrived near mile marker seventeen, he slowed down and looked around. Then he saw something on the side of the road. He parked his car and climbed out of the vehicle. He grabbed a flashlight and switched the light on. And almost immediately, he noticed Sean's body.

"Oh my God!" Uncle Matthew ran to the body that lay motionless on the ground. A bullet wound centered his blood-soaked chest. His lifeless eyes still open with fear.

Uncle Matthew fell onto his knees.

"Oh my God," he breathed.

He stared at the body for a few moments before taking his hand and carefully closing Sean's eyes.

Uncle Matthew glanced up at the path in the forest that stood before him and noticed several footprints in the mud. He wondered if perhaps the people who killed Sean were still in those woods and if they had Ava.

"It's worth a shot," he told himself before standing up and brushing the dirt from his knees.

He headed off into the dark woods, unsure of what he was looking for or what he might find.

Chapter Ten

The sound of the large warehouse door being opened awoke Ava from her sleep. A man and woman approached her both wearing dark clothing.

"What?" Ava asked groggily. She noticed that her stomach felt empty and she was craving any type of food.

"She's ready to see you," the man said.

"Who?" Ava inquired, until her question was answered when another a small group of people entered the building, one man pushing an elderly woman in a wheelchair.

Ava's eyes quickly fell on the woman as she was brought into the light. She looked as if she had escaped death hundreds of times. Wrinkles sprawled all over her face to such an extent that it was hard to notice any other feature on her face. She had light, pale skin and her white, long hair was braided down and around her shoulder.

The room fell quiet. And when the man moved the old woman to where she could look directly at Ava, he stepped aside with the others.

Ava was unsure of what to do. She watched as the lady simply stared at her in silence.

"Are you…Esmerelda?" Ava inquired.

The lady watched her solemnly, until a small smile grew on her cracked lips. "Why, yes. I am."

Ava stared at Esmerelda. This was the woman who created an unthinkable evil, an abomination. And yet she looked so fragile, as if one touch to her skin would make her fall apart.

"A-Are you going to kill me?" Ava stuttered. A million questions ran through her mind, and she needed them all answered before she ran out of time.

"I think you know that I can't do that, now can I?" Esmerelda spoke, "Now, you were promised answers to any questions that you may have, so, go on, ask away."

"I know what you're trying to do," Ava said, suddenly feeling the urge to cry, "I know you want us all to die. But I'm begging you, please don't kill my uncle."

"That's not a question," Esmerelda reminded Ava, "But to answer your request, unfortunately everyone is going to die, so I can't somehow keep your uncle alive while the rest of the population is extinguished. That doesn't make sense, does it? I want *questions,* Ava. Don't test my patience. I'm nice enough to allow this meeting to happen," Esmerelda said raising her voice slightly.

"S-Sorry," Ava glanced at the three people who watched them converse, each were staring at her with a dull expression. "So… how are you still alive? Weren't you supposed to die with Finis?"

"Good question. Well, you see, before your ancestor and her friends were about to seal me in with Finis, I used a spell to transfer my soul to a different body. They didn't know, and it allowed me my freedom, I've been doing that over and over again for the past few centuries."

"Do you plan on doing it again?"

"Why, of course not. We're all going to die soon, remember? That goes for me, too. I would've switched to a nicer, newer body by now. This body is almost useless, but it works well enough."

"Do you still have your magic?"

"Sure, that's how I'm keeping this body from shutting down. Next question."

"If you killed Sean, how is his stone going to be placed into the mountain? Doesn't it have to be placed by an ancestor of the stone's creator?"

"My, you do know your stuff, don't you? Sean is not the only Yorke descendent here in Parkfield; his cousin is more than willing to take his place."

Ava thought for a moment, then a question she had wondered for a while popped into her mind.

"When is this all going to happen?"

Esmerelda leaned in towards Ava as far as she could without falling from her chair and whispered, "Tonight, my dear."

Ava gasped; she felt her heart beat several times quicker. "B-But it's not a blood moon tonight,"

"Haven't you looked? Oh, right, you've been trapped in here this whole time." Esmerelda chuckled. "Well, we injected you with a few drugs, so you've been asleep for about a day."

"A day?" Ava's eyes widened. She felt as if she had perhaps twenty minutes of sleep, not twenty-four hours.

"We didn't want you to get bored while awaiting your fate, or to try something," Esmerelda said smiling.

"Ma'am," a woman spoke from the doorway, "It's time."

"Oh, yes…yes, yes," Esmerelda said ecstatically before turning back to Ava, "I've waited centuries for this moment. It's exciting, don't you think?"

Ava was unable to speak any further.

"I'll take that as a yes. Darren! Take me to Mount Redlock!"

The same man who wheeled her into the room walked quickly to Esmerelda and began pushing her towards the door.

"I'll see you soon, Ava Sinclair!" Esmerelda said, her voice echoed slightly in the dark room.

"Please, you have to understand," Ava said to the others in the room, "This is so crazy. If this works, we will all die."

"Here's your last dose," the man said to Ava as he pulled out another syringe.

"No, please," Ava begged, "don't do this."

The man approached her and swiftly injected the shot into her arm, almost immediately making her drowsy.

"This is a mistake," she said slowly, closing her eyes and falling asleep again.

As Matthew followed the trail, he saw a clearing in the distance. The woods opened up and revealed the old cabin. As he cautiously approached the open front door, he drew his gun. "Police! Ava, are you here?!" he yelled, but only silence followed.

As he entered the cabin, he noticed chairs turned over and fresh footprints everywhere. He pointed his light to the bookshelf and it didn't take long before he noticed a book placed upside down and sticking out a few inches from all the other books, Isabelle Sinclair's diary. He removed it and discovered a piece of ripped paper stuck out from the top. He opened the book to remove the note and read it.

This is what they believe – Ava

"Good work, Ava. That's my girl," he said to himself proudly.

Uncle Matthew walked over to the small table and sat the book down on it. He flipped through the old pages, scanning words every so often, then flipped to the first page to see his namesake.

"Isabelle Sinclair…" he muttered to himself as he began to read the diary quickly and intently.

The more he read, the more he understood.

He as well as Ava were descendants of a witch, Anne Sinclair, who lived here in the 1600's. She was good, as well as the many other witches who lived there. And they thrived on each other and their abilities peacefully, until a witch named Esmerelda destroyed the peace that once lived in Parkfield.

"Finis," he read aloud.

Uncle Matthew continued flipping page after page, gaining more knowledge about the witches that lived among the humans of Parkfield.

"Four stones…"

"A cave…"

"Passed down to each descendent,"

"Abolish the dooming stone…"

He read her last entry before taking the book and scrambling out of the cabin, through the woods and back into his car.

He now knew the truth, or what these people believed to be the truth. He started his car and drove back into town.

The full moon was a deep shade of red rising high in the sky. Instead of the streets being quiet and deserted at this hour, they were flooded with townspeople. Everyone was sitting on benches, watching the moon in awe. Ever since Matthew found Ava's note and read the journal in the broken-down cabin in the woods, he knew that something was seriously wrong in the town of Parkfield.

As he made his way past the busy sidewalks, he noticed how everyone was wearing their nicest clothing and jewelry. Some were crying, while others hugged each other as if saying goodbye.

When he arrived back at the police station, he ran out of his car and into the building.

"Hello? Is anyone here? Jacob, are you here?!" Uncle Matthew couldn't see anyone in the lobby, not even at the front desk.

He walked around the fully-lit room; it looked as if everyone just dropped what they were doing and left.

"What is up with this crazy town?" Uncle Matthew breathed, putting his hands on his hips.

He heard the front door open and quickly turned around locking eyes with a frightened Jacob.

"Jacob!" Uncle Matthew angrily shouted.

"Matthew," Jacob swallowed, cowering near the doorway.

"I just found the chief's body near the highway like you said. How the hell did you he would be there?" he yelled, balling his fists.

"I-I wasn't supposed to tell," Jacob said.

"Who told you not to? You're a damn police officer, Jacob! It's your job!"

"This was different, this *is* different."

"Who killed Sean?!" Uncle Matthew walked over to Jacob and grabbed his shirt, yanking him forward. "Who did it?!"

"I-I don't know!" Jacob's eyes were filled with fear.

"You don't know, huh?" Uncle Matthew let go of Jacob's collared shirt which made Jacob stumble back outside. "How do you not know? I found that cabin back in the woods and I know Ava was there at some point. I'm sure you were too, so who killed Sean and where is Ava?!"

"I-I was far back on the trail on the way out when it happened. S-someone else shot him, I don't know who. There were so many of us. And Ava got away so I don't know where she is either."

"So, there were lots of people there? Who were they?"

"Just some townspeople, that's all!" Jacob confessed.

"And what were you all doing there? That cabin looked like it was ransacked pretty recently."

"Yes, that was us, but we didn't do anything wrong there." Jacob hung his head.

"Answer me truthfully! I found a note from Ava inside the cabin in an old diary," Uncle Matthew said as he reached into his pocket and pulled out a slip of paper, "I wasn't sure what she meant, but maybe you will."

"What does it say?" Jacob asked.

"*This is what they believe,*" Uncle Matthew read aloud. "Do you believe is all this mumbo jumbo about stones and witches and the end of the world?"

"Uh, no," Jacob lied.

"Are you sure?" Uncle Matthew questioned him.

"I'm sure, I promise. I wouldn't lie to you, Matthew."

"That's the funniest thing I've heard all day. This town seems to be nothing but lies."

Uncle Matthew chuckled, placing the note back in his pocket.

Jacob sensed the urgency and worry in Matthew, so out of sympathy he decided to answer the question he had asked the most.

"If you want to find your girl, I would head to the peak of Mount Redlock. I can't guarantee you'll be safe or that it will be a good idea, but you'll find Ava there."

Matthew locked eyes with Jacob one final time before running back out to the parking lot.

"Please don't make me do this!" a girl next to Ava screamed. She jerked around as two men held her, forcing her to stand before the face of the mountaintop.

Ava as well as a young man and this woman were held tightly. Another man in line with them was guarded but not held, he wore a smile on his face.

That must be Sean's cousin, Ava thought to herself.

The two men that held Ava's arms tightened their grip as Ava winced.

People wearing long, black hooded robes crowded around them. Some held torches while others held flashlights. Ava turned her head back to see a glimpse of Parkfield, all lit up and active. She wished she had just stayed in her room.

"She's here!" Ava heard someone yell.

Everyone turned to their right to see two large men carrying a wheelchair, one on each side. They carefully made their way up the rocky path leading to the top of Mount Redlock before setting the chair down where the ground leveled off. Then one of them pushed the chair into the silent, mesmerized crowd. Esmerelda had arrived.

They wheeled her right in front of the cave entrance where Finis supposedly waited. She then faced the crowd.

"Welcome, all," she said smiling to the silent crowd, "You've all waited years for this, and now our time has come. Each descendent standing here will place their ancestor's stone into the mountain face behind me one at a time."

She glanced at Ava and the three other ancestors before continuing.

"Once they have placed their stones in the mountain, man's putrid existence on earth will come to an end. A new world awaits all of us!" she cackled.

"No!" the woman next to Ava yelled, "Please, I have a family! I don't want to do this!"

"Please, there's no need for this! Let us go!" yelled the young man as he tried to free himself from his restrainers. Ava watched in horror as the people around them laughed and cheered.

"Quiet!" Esmerelda ordered the people around Ava. Everyone quieted down instantly. "The blood moon is at its peak," she said as she looked up and smiled, "It's time."

"Please," the woman next to Ava sobbed as she fell to her knees, "I don't want to die."

"It's for the best, my dear," Esmerelda said, "You'll understand eventually. Now, bring me the stones!"

Hoots and hollers broke from the cult members as they waved their torches high, entrancing Ava with their dancing flames.

A man handed a small, ornate box to Esmerelda and she opened it slowly. Though the lid hid the contents from the onlookers' view, everyone knew that the infamous gemstones were inside as a soft glow of several colors lit up the old woman's ragged face.

She reached into the box and picked up a stone that was mostly clear with glimmers of red. She examined it between her fingertips, entranced by the glow. Holding it high, she said, "Now, will the rightful heir of this stone please come forward?"

No one approached.

The boy that appeared to be only a few years older than Ava began crying incessantly. One of the two men holding him spoke.

"It's his. It's Stephen's."

A devious smile appeared on Esmerelda's lips as she moved her fingers, signifying that she wanted him to be brought over.

The two men pulled him over to Esmerelda, his knees dragging in the dirt. His sobs could be heard by everyone until the moment when people began to cheer, drowning out his cries. He was placed right before Esmerelda.

"Hello, Stephen," the old witch said as she looked down at him, "This is your ancestor's stone, isn't it?" she looked at the small, glowing stone in her hand.

"Yes," he sniffed. His voice was hoarse and defeated sounding.

"Well then," Esmerelda said as she placed her cold hand underneath his chin and lifted his head so that they had eye-contact, "whenever you're ready. Find its place in the mountain."

Tears streamed down his tired face as Esmerelda placed the stone into his palm. The same two men who held him earlier placed their hands underneath Stephen's arms and lifted him onto his feet, pushing him past Esmerelda and towards the mountain face.

Stephen stumbled towards the closed-up cave, immediately locating the small holes in front of him. They formed a square pattern.

"Well?" the witch asked from behind him, "What are you waiting for? One way or another you will fulfill your destiny."

"I-I can't," he stuttered with fear.

One of the men who helped carry Esmerelda approached him with eyes of pure evil. He grabbed Stephen by the throat and lifted him off of his feet.

Stephen gagged multiple times, hitting the man's large arms as hard as he could. The scary man placed him back down on the ground.

"All right...I'll...I'll do it," he said, attempting to regain his loss of breath.

Ava watched in horror as Stephen approached the boulder once more and stared intently at each divot.

"Try each one," the old woman demanded, "but hurry, we don't have much time."

Stephen nodded and placed the stone in the first hole, but it didn't fit.

"Try another!" someone yelled from the large group of people.

Stephen's hand shook as he guided the gemstone to another hole, placing it inside accordingly. This time, it fit. The hole and stone were like magnets, bound for each other to connect.

Cheers broke out from the crowd. Esmerelda applauded accordingly. Stephen turned around to face the group of people cheering in his honor, horrified by what he had done.

Once the applause died down, Esmerelda merely smiled. "Congratulations, Stephen. But unfortunately, we have no use for you anymore."

"W-what?" he asked.

"Will," Esmerelda said to the same scary man who approached him earlier.

"No! Please! No!" Stephen screamed as Will picked him up and carried him to the edge of the cliff.

"Thank you, Stephen. Your destiny is now officially fulfilled," Esmerelda said sweetly.

Will then tossed Stephen off the mountain; his screams echoed until they replaced by a sickening thud from far below.

It was dead silent for a few moments, until the crowd around the descendants began to roar again with excitement. Ava glanced at the other heirs with dread.

"Well!" Esmerelda clapped her hands a couple times, bringing everyone's attention back to her. "Who's next?"

Uncle Matthew drove up Mount Redlock as far as the road would allow before parking his car and getting out. The moon lit up the ground with an eerie blood-red color which was occasionally covered up by the tall, swaying forest trees.

Once he got out, he heard the screams and cheers coming from atop the mountain, the peak flickering with a warm glow.

Uncle Matthew struggled as he scrambled up the mountain, stumbling over rocks and crashing through small trees until he reached the summit. There a crowd was gathered, and he saw a familiar face in the flickering glow of the torches.

Ava.

Matthew drew his gun and badge.

"Ava!" Uncle Matthew yelled as he fired his gun into the air.

Everyone gasped as they turned to look at him. The cheering had suddenly stopped, and everyone was now dead silent.

"Police! Nobody make any sudden moves!"

The people moved out of Uncle Matthew's way as he pushed past them towards Ava.

"Ava, look, I know what's going on. These people are crazy. We need to leave," he said boldly.

"Uncle Matthew, you need to go," Ava breathed, "Now."

"You must be Matthew, correct?" Esmerelda spoke up.

Uncle Matthew turned around pointing his gun at the old woman.

"Let my daughter go," Uncle Matthew demanded.

"I can't do that," she spoke, "that would ruin some very important plans. You need to drop your weapon, detective."

One of the cult members produced a gun, grabbed Ava and put it against her head.

"Put it down or she dies!" he snarled.

Matthew stopped and slowly placed his gun on the ground which was quickly retrieved by a woman from the crowd. Two men grabbed Matthew immediately.

"Don't you dare harm her; I know what this is about. I don't believe any of it but you lunatics seem to!" Matthew said before taking a deep breath.

"Tell you what," Uncle Matthew continued, "I'm an ancestor too, aren't I? A Sinclair descendent? Take me instead."

"Uncle Matthew, no!" Ava screamed as she attempted to break free from the men holding her, but they held tight.

"Hmm," Esmerelda mused, "I suppose that's a fair trade."

A sigh of relief came from Uncle Matthew.

"Actually," Esmerelda began again, "I'd rather you witness your precious girl die." She smiled a devilish grin.

"You monster!" Uncle Matthew yelled.

The two men restraining Uncle Matthew pulled him aside into the crowd.

"Let go of me, now!" he screamed.

"Ava, I suppose this makes it your turn," Esmerelda said.

Ava gulped as she was suddenly shoved by the two men who had held her and landed before Esmerelda on the ground.

"Out of all the stones," Esmerelda said picking up the purple stone from the box, "this one hass always been my favorite."

She placed the gemstone in Ava's hand.

"Please don't make me do this," Ava sobbed, her head hung low to the ground.

"You have no choice," the old woman spoke.

"Don't do this, Ava!" Uncle Matthew yelled as tears streamed down his face.

"Oh, shut up!" Esmerelda snapped, "Hurry up now, Ava. We still have two more to go."

Suddenly, a familiar fragrance entered Ava's nose. Lavender tea.

She paused.

"Could I at least look at the city one last time?" Ava sniffled, "Before everything is destroyed."

"Well, I suppose you can, but hurry up." Esmerelda scoffed.

Ava stood up and turned to Parkfield. Lights still seeped from buildings illuminating trees and rows of cars. Everything down there seemed at peace, unaware of what was about to happen. Even with the red glow of the blood moon, Ava noticed how peaceful everything looked.

A stronger sense of the aroma of lavender tea surged through her senses, it was almost unbearable. She then returned to the thought that she had focused on ever since she had been dragged to the peak of this mountain.

"Note the following words carefully: the only way to abolish the dooming stone is to die with it in your possession."

Ava turned to look at her uncle. Tears made everything blurry, but she nonetheless recognized his appearance in the torchlights and smiled.

"I love you," she said.

He watched her with tears in his eyes.

"What are you doing?" Esmerelda inquired, her voice suddenly raising with concern.

Within a split second, Ava sprinted towards the edge of the cliff, shoving people past her and dodging others. With the gemstone still grasped in her hand, she knew that this was the right thing to do.

"Stop her!" Esmerelda shrieked.

'Ava, NO!" screamed Uncle Matthew.

Men ran after her, quickly catching up, grabbing her clothing, but she was on a mission and shook loose. Will was inches from grasping her but he wasn't quick enough.

Ava leaped off the cliff.

She could hear screams from the crowd, but they grew more distant the further she fell.

Death was a concept so frightening that she couldn't imagine bearing it. Peace and death were two words she believed were complete opposites, which was why the idea of dying was a horrifying one. She didn't want to die, nor did she want to leave this world and its many gifts. But she knew that the end was inevitable, so she closed her eyes and let the moment take her.

She allowed herself to feel peace. The peace in knowing that she had just saved the world.

Chapter Eleven

Ava opened her eyes.

She found herself in a hospital bed. Lots of tubes and wires were attached to her and she felt very drowsy. She looked before her and saw a familiar window. It had light blue curtains and a tree branch was outside, gently waving in the outdoor breeze.

She was in a very small room, it all seemed familiar. She looked to her left and saw both of her parents sitting in large, padded chairs. Her dad was asleep and her mom was reading a book. Next to her mom was a steaming cup of lavender tea.

"Mom? Dad?" Ava asked in confusion.

Her mother looked up, shocked, and grabbed Ava's hand.

"Ava? Can you hear me?! William, she's awake!" her mother shouted with tears in her eyes.

"Yes, Mom…I'm here," Ava said in a very weak voice.

Her father shot out of his chair, came over and touched her hand. He looked as if he was going to cry too but had a big smile on his face.

"Ava are you okay?" he asked.

Ava nodded and smiled.

"Nurse! She's awake!!" her mother yelled out of the hospital room.

A woman in a white uniform ran in the room and over to Ava.

"Oh my gosh. I can't believe this!" exclaimed the nurse.

The woman called for doctors and nurses while Ava's parents stood in disbelief.

After a few examinations, the doctors and nurses left Ava's room. One of the doctors asked her parents to step outside of the room with him. A few minutes later, her parents walked back inside, tears streaming down their faces.

"What's wrong?" Ava asked, "What's happening?"

"Nothing's wrong. You're okay," her father said smiling and wiping the tears from his face.

"We are just so glad you finally woke up," her mother said.

"Wait, I'm so confused," Ava said, "I thought you both died in that car wreck!"

"After the wreck we were both knocked unconscious, but someone saw what happened and called an ambulance. We were all taken to the hospital. Your father and I were banged up pretty bad and I broke my arm, but you, you fell into a coma."

"I was in a coma? For how long?"

"For…six years," Ava's mom said as she began to sob, "Six long years."

"No…no, I-I was in Harvard, and Uncle Matthew was my guardian, and we were working on a case together, and, and there was an evil cult in Parkfield that was after me…and…"

"Ava, Ava…that was all a dream," Ava's dad sighed.

"We were heading to Parkfield when the wreck happened," her mother said.

"I can't believe it. This is all so crazy!! I was forced to go up to a cliff with this magic crystal that I was supposed to place into a mountain to unleash an evil entity before they killed me! Uncle Matthew was there trying to save me, and he even said he'd take my place and sacrifice himself for me. Where's Uncle Matthew? I want to talk to him. He and I had the craziest adventure together!"

Her parents sadly looked at each other.

"Oh, Ava," her mom said slowly, "Uncle Matthew died soon after the car accident."

Ava sat up in shock.

"What?"

"He was shot while on duty…" she said.

Tears filled Ava's eyes.

"Uncle Matthew is dead?" Ava choked, "I…was just with him."

"Ava I am so sorry," said her father on the verge of sobbing, "It was so hard losing my brother, especially with you being in a coma as well, but…you are awake now and that is such a blessing for all of us."

They all three hugged as doctors entered the room to continue to monitor Ava and her condition.

Later that night, Ava sat up in bed while her parents slept in the chairs in her room. She was tired but couldn't sleep, she was afraid that she might not wake up again, even though the doctors said that wouldn't happen. She couldn't believe how her entire reality changed. Six years of her life weren't even real. And her dear Uncle Matthew is dead.

Ava looked out of the window in front of her. The sky was a cloudless sunset. Ava remembered this window…light blue curtains, a tree branch right outside, she saw it in her dreams. There was a bird that would land on that tree branch in her dreams. Ava waited, she wondered if the bird would show up. Finally, a small dove landed on the branch, it looked around until its eyes met with Ava's. It flew onto the window sill and stared at her. They both watched each other for several seconds until it flew off.

Ava smiled as she peacefully fell asleep.